"You don't have a corner on pain and suffering."

The quiet statement set Gabe's anger off like a torch. "What do you know about pain? You sit in that clinic and hand out lollipops to kids and tell your adult patients to take two aspirin and go to the emergency room."

Lana paled. "You're wrong. I know a lot about pain." She leaned forward, and when she spoke, her voice was low, but he heard every word. "I know what it's like to want to slap the next well-meaning person who gives you a pitying look and then turns away because he or she doesn't know what to say. I know what it's like to drink yourself into oblivion, hoping, praying you'll forget. But you can't. There's not enough liquor in the world to drown that pain."

He started to speak, but she held up a hand and continued, her eyes holding a sorrow that went fathoms deep. "I know what it's like to look at a bottle of pills and think about how damn easy it would be to take them all and escape that way." She looked away. "Trust me, I know. Better than you do."

He was an idiot. "I'm sorry," he said gruffly. "When I screw up I don't do it halfway. What happened?"

Expressionless, she stared at him for a long moment. "None of your business."

Dear Reader,

Ever since Gabe Randolph, the hero of *That Night in Texas*, first walked onto the page in *Trouble in Texas*, I've wanted to write his story.

Gabe is a man who's always been sure of what he wants and has been lucky enough to get it. Until an accident one terrible night changes his whole future. Dr. Lana McCoy also knows how one night can change a person forever. When she comes to Aransas City to start over, she has no intention of including a man in her life. Then she meets Gabe, who she comes to find has more in common with her than she could ever have imagined. Each has been burned, so these two wary survivors ignore the attraction pulling them together. But a passion too strong to be denied will teach them both that they don't have to let one night–no matter how traumatic–define the rest of their lives. I hope you'll enjoy watching them fall in love along the way.

I love to hear from readers. Write me at P.O. Box 131704, Tyler, TX 75713-1704. Or e-mail evegaddybooks@cox.net. And visit my Web site at www.evegaddy.net.

Sincerely,

Eve Gaddy

THAT NIGHT IN TEXAS

Eve Gaddy

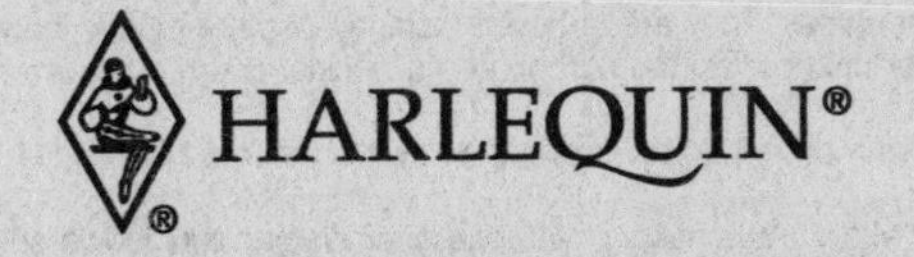

TORONTO • NEW YORK • LONDON
AMSTERDAM • PARIS • SYDNEY • HAMBURG
STOCKHOLM • ATHENS • TOKYO • MILAN • MADRID
PRAGUE • WARSAW • BUDAPEST • AUCKLAND

ISBN 0-373-71313-4

THAT NIGHT IN TEXAS

This edition published by arrangement with Harlequin Books S.A.

www.eHarlequin.com

Printed in U.S.A.

Books by Eve Gaddy

HARLEQUIN SUPERROMANCE

903–COWBOY COME HOME
962–FULLY ENGAGED
990–A MAN OF HIS WORD
1031–TROUBLE IN TEXAS
1090–A MARRIAGE MADE IN TEXAS
1122–CASEY'S GAMBLE
1276–SOMEWHERE IN TEXAS

Acknowledgments

Many thanks to Sergeant Matthew Lohenitz of the City of Easton Police Department for patiently answering my many questions. Also, my thanks to Rob Preece and Lisa Montgomery. Your presentation was not only great, it was the turning point for me when I was really struggling with this book. Thanks so much.

Dedication

This book is for my children, Diana and Chris, and my soon to be son-in-law, Russ. For my daughter, Diana, who as I write this is preparing to marry her own hero. Diana, I wish for you and Russ all the love and happiness you deserve in your new life together. For my son, Chris, who as I write this is preparing to graduate from high school. Chris, you've made us very proud. I hope your college years bring you knowledge, friendship and most of all, happiness. And always, for my husband, Bob. I love you all.

CHAPTER ONE

"SO ARE YOU coming to dinner Saturday night? Best barbecue you'll ever taste. I'm cooking."

Dr. Lana McCoy looked up at the man lounging in her office doorway. "That depends on whether you're trying to set me up with someone or not," she replied.

Blond and handsome, her new partner was also very happily married. She'd known and worked with Jay Kincaid in an emergency room back in California, before he moved to Aransas City, a small town on the Texas coast.

He grinned. "I'm not, but my wife probably is."

"Then no. Thanks, but no thanks."

He considered her a moment. "What do you have against men, Lana?"

"I have nothing against men. I just don't want to date them."

After her divorce was finalized, she'd started looking for a new job, a new life, but she hadn't found anything suitable. Then she'd run into Jay at a medical conference and mentioned she was looking to relocate. Next thing she knew, she was on her way to Texas to work with Jay and his partner, Tim Kramer, at their medical clinic.

She'd come to the sleepy little town of Aransas City for peace. And though she'd only been here a few short weeks, she thought she might have finally found her new home. If only she could convince her partners and their wives and nearly everyone else she'd met that she was perfectly happy being single and had no intention of changing that status.

Jay rubbed his chin. "Okay. I'll tell Gail. But would you come if you knew it was just a get-together and we promised not to try to set you up?"

She smiled at him. "Yes." She didn't mind making new friends. It was dating she had an aversion to. "Now go away, I have work to do."

"Great. Seven o'clock," he said, and left her.

By Saturday she was having second thoughts. Still, why shouldn't she go? she asked herself as she dressed for the barbecue in cool linen slacks and a pale blue sleeveless silk blouse. If she was going to make Aransas City her home, then she should go out and meet people. What better way to do so than a casual get-together? She'd already met Jay's wife, Gail, and liked her, and she knew that Gail and Jay had lots of family and friends in the area.

Of course, there would probably be single men at the party, but as long as no one tried to set her up, she could cope. She'd discouraged men before. Most of them didn't stick around long enough to see if they could break the barrier she put up between them. Those who did, gave up after a few tries and moved on to women who took less effort. Which was exactly what she wanted.

"MAMA MIA, who's the hot blonde walking this way?" Gabe Randolph asked his brother-in-law. She wasn't just hot, she was smokin'.

Standing over the barbecue grill in his backyard, Jay flipped a burger, then turned to see who Gabe was talking about. "That's my new partner. Lana McCoy."

"She's your new partner?" He looked at Jay, then back at the blonde. "Whoa. You've been holding out on me. So, tell me the bad news. Is she married?"

Jay shook his head, a smile playing around his mouth. "Divorced."

"Okay, so what's the problem? Why hasn't Gail introduced her to me?"

Lana McCoy was single, beautiful and a doctor. The kind of woman Gabe's sister would consider perfect for him, never mind that he wouldn't have much in common with a brainiac. Still, brainy or not, anyone who looked like this woman was definitely worth getting to know. But Gail hadn't said a word so there must be a problem.

Ever since his brother Cam had married Delilah

a few months before, his two sisters, Gail and Cat, not to mention Cam's wife, had been throwing every female they could find at him. They weren't going to be happy until every damn one of their relatives was married. Of course, that wasn't going to happen with him, but he didn't mind going out with the women they kept finding for him.

Jay flipped another burger. "I told Gail she couldn't. To get Lana to come tonight, I had to promise her we wouldn't try to set her up with anyone."

"So she doesn't like blind dates. Who does?"

Jay shook his head and glanced at Gabe. Lana had stopped to talk to Cat. "From what I gathered, she doesn't like dates period."

Gabe tilted his head, considering her. "She doesn't date? Why not?"

"Beats me," Jay said with a shrug. "Guess you'll have to find out."

Well, maybe I will, he thought, watching her. He drank some of his beer. If she really wasn't interested, she'd shoot him down, but big deal. He'd been shot down before and no doubt would be again. She was talking to Delilah now so he made his way over to the two of them.

"Gabe," Delilah said when she caught sight of him. She gave him a hug and smiled at him. "We haven't seen you in the restaurant in weeks."

"Start of the busy season," he said. And, thank God, business had been booming lately. "I'm

Gabe Randolph," he said to the blonde, holding out a hand.

"Lana McCoy. I'm Jay's and Tim's new partner." Though she shook hands she dropped his quickly.

"You know, Gabe, it's lucky you're here," Delilah said. "Lana was just saying how she'd never been deep-sea fishing. Or even fishing period." She turned to Lana and smiled. "Gabe runs a charter fishing service. He's just the person to show you the ropes." She winked at Gabe. "I see someone I need to talk to. You'll entertain Lana, won't you, Gabe?" She walked off, leaving them alone.

Lana didn't look very happy about that. *Man, she's one classy number,* he thought. Long, straight, pale blond hair spilled to her shoulders. Her eyes were ocean-blue and right now as frosty as an ice-cold mug of beer. Her mouth was generous, unpainted and frowning. He wanted to see her smile.

"Sorry, she's not very subtle," he said.

"Subtle?" She looked blank for a moment, then frowned again. "Oh. I take it you're single."

"Free as a bird," he confirmed cheerfully. "And obviously, so are you. Do you really want to go fishing or did Delilah dream that up?"

"No, I did mention I'd like to try it sometime."

"Great. How does tomorrow sound?"

"I don't know. How much does it cost?"

He smiled. "For you, nothing."

"That wouldn't be right. I can't ask you to take me fishing for free."

To any other woman he'd have said, "Make it a date," but according to Jay that wouldn't work with her. "It's no big deal. Think of it like a welcome gift for newcomers. How about it, Lana? Will you let me take you fishing tomorrow?"

She seemed to consider that for a moment, then something like regret flashed across her face. "Thanks, but I really can't."

He knew he should drop the subject, but the devil inside him made him ask, "Can't or won't?"

Their gazes met and held before she dropped hers. After a moment she said, "I don't date."

"We don't have to call it a date. Just a little fishing."

"You don't have to call it a date for it to be a date. And going fishing on your boat sounds like a date to me."

"Nope." He shook his head. "There's where you're wrong. If I was asking you on a date, I'd have done it completely differently."

"How would—" She stopped and held up a hand. "No, don't tell me. How did I get into this conversation?"

"Well, I asked you if you wanted to go fishing and you said you—"

She interrupted him by laughing. "Stop. You're not going to get me to change my mind by making me laugh."

"Worth a try."

"Are you always this persistent?"

He couldn't help smiling. "No. But most women I meet aren't as pretty as you are."

Something hit him hard in the middle of his back. He stumbled forward and his beer pitched out of his hand. Splattering all over Lana McCoy's pretty silk shirt.

Gabe turned around ready to rip someone's head off, only to find his niece Mel and a little friend of hers. He swallowed the curse that had been on his lips.

"I'm sorry, Uncle Gabe," she said, looking younger than her ten years. "I was showing Patty my cartwheel. We're both on the Middle School Cheer Squad and it's our new move."

Middle School Cheer Squad? Middle school? How had that happened? She'd been five years old just last week, hadn't she? God, he felt old.

"Tell the lady you're sorry, Mel. I spilled my drink on her."

"Uh-oh," she said, looking at Lana who was ineffectually wiping beer off her shirt. "I'm sorry, ma'am. I didn't mean to. Are you mad with me?"

Gabe was ready to step in, but it wasn't necessary. The irritation had left Lana's face and she smiled at the little girls. "No, of course not. It was an accident." She held out a hand. "I'm Lana McCoy."

When she smiled like that…oh, man, it almost made him forget his name.

They talked to the girls for a few minutes, then Mel and her friend ran off. Lana looked at him. "You thought I was going to yell at her."

"The thought crossed my mind," he admitted. "And I couldn't really blame you." Her shirt was soaked. She was going to smell like a brewery. "I really am sorry. I'll pay for the dry-cleaning. But for now, let's go ask Gail to lend you a shirt. Mel's her daughter, so it seems only fair."

"I don't—"

"Yes, you do," he interrupted. "You can't drive home smelling like you drank a six-pack. If a cop stops you, he'll throw you in jail in a heartbeat." He started walking toward the house and after a moment she followed.

"Gabe?" She hurried to catch up with him, so he slowed just a bit to let her. As they walked, she kept darting worried glances at him. "About what I said, it's not you. I'm just…um…not interested in dating."

"Okay."

"I don't want you to think…well, that it's personal. It's not."

"Okay."

"I'm sure you're a perfectly nice man, but I just don't…date."

He continued walking toward the house. "Lana, it's no big deal. I invited you fishing and you said no. End of story. You don't need to explain it to me."

She didn't say anything else. He opened the

kitchen door to let her walk inside. "I'll go get Gail and tell her what happened."

"Thanks." She smiled at him. "I appreciate it."

"No problem." He hesitated before he left, then decided what the hell. "Can I ask you something?"

"What?"

"Is this ban on dating a permanent thing?"

She stared at him a moment. "I don't know," she said slowly. Then she added, "Probably."

At least she hadn't said yes, he thought philosophically as he went to find his sister.

After that he didn't talk to Lana again until late in the evening. The party was winding down and he was ready to leave. He was a little surprised when Lana stopped him on his way out.

"Would you mind if I walked out with you?"

"Sure." He wondered why. Maybe she'd changed her mind. He watched her say her goodbyes and thank Jay and Gail for inviting her. Nah, he couldn't get that lucky.

He walked her to her car, a candy-apple-red Porsche. "Nice ride."

"Thanks. I like it." She had her keys out and was surveying the street, looking all around. Her key ring had one of those pepper spray canisters hanging from it. Obviously she was a city girl. Aransas City didn't have much crime. She unlocked the door and he opened it for her. "Thanks for walking me out," she said, and got in.

"Not a problem. Drive safely," he said, and shut her door.

So much for her changing her mind. A balmy spring night, a beautiful woman and him. And they were both going home alone.

"Bummer," he muttered and got in his truck.

LANA WOUND UP following Gabe Randolph through town. He drove, not surprisingly, a big black pickup. She had no idea where he lived, but there weren't a lot of choices in Aransas City. For all she knew, he lived down the street from her.

Gabe Randolph had been…interesting. Not what she'd expected. In fact, she'd been more than a little intrigued by him. And she couldn't figure out why, when she hadn't been intrigued by a man in ages. Those dark eyes, dark hair and go-to-hell good looks couldn't be the only reasons, could they? Surely she wasn't that shallow. Or was she?

Could be, she thought with a smile. But there was more to his appeal than that. He'd taken her refusal in stride, hadn't made her feel like a heel the way some men did. And he hadn't made her feel stupid about her fumbling explanation, either.

All he'd done was ask her if the dating ban was permanent. She'd had a crazy urge to tell him no. Thank God, she hadn't. She knew from bitter experience that dating just didn't work. Not for her, anyway.

She pulled up behind him, at the light at Main and

Redbird. The only one in town. The lack of traffic still astounded her. As did the slow pace of the small town, for that matter. After the frenetic pace of Los Angeles, Aransas City didn't seem quite real.

The light changed while she was daydreaming, and Gabe's truck pulled out into the intersection. She put her foot on the gas and started forward when she glimpsed movement out of the corner of her eye. Braking, she turned her head, and saw a huge truck barreling out of the darkness, heading straight at Gabe's truck.

She sat frozen, staring at it with her mouth agape. *Oh, my God, it's not going to stop.* Before she could even touch the horn, there was a horrendous crash of shrieking metal and broken glass as one truck plowed into the side of the other.

An engine revved. She hadn't moved, hadn't even comprehended what had happened when the second truck backed up and peeled out, tires screaming. She watched it go in horror, then found her purse and took down the license number, grabbed her cell phone and dialed 9-1-1 before flinging open her door. She ran to Gabe's truck. *Please, God, let him be alive.*

The operator answered as she reached the heap of twisted metal that had once been a shiny black pickup. She gave what details she could and hung up quickly. The front end and part of his door was all but totaled, and there was no way she could open that door. She ran around to the other side, opened the door and crawled in.

"Gabe, can you hear me?" The air bag had deflated and she reached for his neck, trying to find a pulse. He groaned when she touched him. "Thank God. Are you conscious?"

"What—happened—shit," he said on a cry of pain. "My leg—can't move—"

"Don't try," she rushed to say. Keeping him still and as calm as possible was important. "EMS is on its way. You need to be still so you don't injure yourself further."

He leaned his head back, the muscles in his neck cording. "Can't—God—hurts."

"I know. Help will be here soon." She wished she could do something, could at least assess his condition, but she didn't have any of the instruments she needed to do that. Best she could do was wait for EMS. In the meantime, she would try to keep him quiet and still.

"Where does it hurt?" She could see him, though not clearly, in the light thrown off by the street lamps. His forehead was bleeding. Broken glass, she thought, because she knew he hadn't gone through the windshield. The airbag had done its job. And he wore his seat belt, which was probably why he was alive right now.

"Gabe, are you still with me?"

"Yeah. Side…hurts. My leg. Hurts. Feels… weird."

She looked down at his left leg. What little she could see wasn't good. It was wedged against the crushed door and covered in blood. "Hang in there. You're going to be fine." He sounded groggy. Probably going into shock. She took his hand and squeezed it. Where the hell was the ambulance? Or at least a cop? It seemed like hours had passed since the accident. Was he going to bleed out before they arrived?

"So…am I—gonna die?"

"No, of course not." She had no way of knowing how serious his injuries were, but she wasn't going to tell him that.

"Really…hurts," he said again, then lapsed into silence.

She kept holding his hand, for lack of anything more constructive to do, and silently cursed the emergency team for taking so long to arrive.

"Why…so nice…" he said after a moment.

"Why am I being nice to you?"

"Yeah. Not dying."

If the situation hadn't been so desperate, she'd have smiled at the comment. "You don't have to be dying for me to be nice to you."

"Coulda…fooled me."

The blessed sound of sirens filled the air. "You're going to be fine, Gabe. The ambulance is here."

A few moments later the police, an ambulance and a fire truck arrived together. She stood aside and watched them extract Gabe from the truck and place him on the backboard. They started an IV and then one of the techs motioned for her to come over.

She walked over and took Gabe's hand. She couldn't help looking at his leg. It was worse than she'd first thought, a compound fracture—she could see the bone sticking out through the skin. They were trying to stop the bleeding and apparently not having an easy time. She lifted her gaze and saw one of the techs give a barely perceptible shake of his head. *Not good,* his expression said.

"You're okay now," she said to Gabe. "They're going to get you to the hospital right away."

His eyes filled with pain and cloudy with shock, met hers. "Thanks." He let go of her hand and they loaded him into the back of the ambulance.

From her comments as they worked to get him out, the officer at the scene, Maggie Barnes, knew Gabe well. She watched the ambulance go, then turned to Lana. "I have to call his family. He's in bad shape, isn't he?"

"Yes, he is," Lana said.

Maggie, her expression hardening, said, "If I can find out who did this, it's going to be a pleasure to put him in jail."

"I can help you there," Lana said. "I have the license number of the truck that hit him."

CHAPTER TWO

Three months later

GABE SAT in the orthopedist's waiting room and checked his watch for the fifth time. He was sick and tired of hospitals. He was sick and tired of doctors. And he was really, really sick and tired of being a cripple.

He'd made progress. According to the physical therapist, remarkable progress, considering…

No one ever finished that sentence, but Gabe knew what they meant. Considering what a freaking mess his leg had been after the accident, he was doing well.

Personally, he didn't consider still being on crutches after three months a boatload of progress.

Fifteen minutes later they took him back to an exam room. His new set of X-rays were hanging on the view box. Dr. Black looked at them without saying much, then poked and prodded him, again, asked him to move his leg, move his knee, again… Same old stuff that happened every time he came in. He didn't see the point. Finally the doctor told him to get dressed and come into his office.

Gabe wasn't sure he liked the sound of that. He took a seat in one of the side chairs, carefully arranging his leg so it was in the least uncomfortable position. No position was entirely comfortable. In fact, his leg throbbed like hell eighty-five percent of the time.

"So, what's the verdict? When am I going to get off the crutches and when can I go back to work?"

Dr. Black folded his hands together on his desk. "No one can tell you absolutely. Your physical therapist says you're progressing well. You won't need the crutches much longer."

"A couple of weeks." If he was lucky. Which meant never, if his luck ran the way it usually did.

"You're doing nicely, Gabe. Your injuries, particularly to the knee, were extensive."

"Yeah, I know. But that doesn't pay my bills. I'm self-employed. I don't have disability insurance or workman's comp, Doc. When can I expect to go back to work?"

Dr. Black looked surprised. "You didn't get a settlement from the driver of the other car?"

Gabe laughed humorlessly. "Son of a bitch was driving with a suspended license and no insurance. Can't squeeze blood out of a turnip." But at least they'd found him, thanks to Lana McCoy writing down his license plate. “Bottom line is, I need to get back to work. How about it, Doc? How much longer am I going to be out of commission?”

“We need to talk,” Dr. Black said.

Gabe stared at the doctor. He knew he didn’t like the sound of that.

“Have you ever considered another career?” Dr. Black asked him.

“No. And I’m not going to now. Why should I?”

“Like I said, your injuries were extensive. Rehabilitation is not a fast process in some cases.” He looked at him and added, “You’re almost certainly going to be looking at more surgery on your leg.”

Gabe had known that was a possibility but no one had stated it so bluntly. “But then I’ll be all right.”

“We hope so. That’s our goal.”

“But you can’t guarantee it.”

“I can’t guarantee you won’t limp, but you should regain most of your mobility. Eventually you might need an artificial knee, but given your age, we don’t want to go that route unless we have to.”

“Time frame, Doc. Can you give me some idea of how long before my leg’s back to normal?” More surgery meant more recovery time, physical therapy, everything he’d been going through for the past three months. The doctor looked uncomfortable, but Gabe didn’t care about that. “The truth, Doc. I need to know so I can plan what I’m going to do to get by.”

"Two years. Possibly more. But be aware, that's an estimate. It could be less."

Gabe just stared at him. Two years. Or more. And even then, his leg might never be back to normal. He might never be back to what he was before the accident. And even if he did get most of his mobility back, he couldn't afford to wait that long. He would have to sell his boat, and the sooner the better.

HE DIDN'T KNOW how he made it out of the office without getting sick. He shut the office door behind him and leaned against the wall, struggling to make sense of the words. Two years. Maybe more. He kept hearing them, repeated in an endless loop.

"Gabe?"

He looked up at the sound of the female voice. Just what he didn't want, to see anyone he knew.

"It's Lana McCoy," she said, looking at him closely. "Are you all right?"

"Peachy. And I know who you are." How could he forget? He hadn't seen her since the night of the accident. She'd come by to see him a couple of times while he was in the hospital, but he'd refused visitors. If he could have thrown his family out, he would have done it. But while he had to suffer them, he didn't have to be on display to anyone else.

God, she was pretty. Walking along as if she didn't have a care in the world. He turned his head and hoped she'd take the hint. She didn't.

"Maybe you should sit down. I don't mean to be pushy but you don't look very good."

He turned his head around to look at her. "Neither do you." That was a lie if he'd ever spoken one. Her pale blond hair looked soft and shiny, the kind of hair that begged you to touch to see if it was as baby-soft as it looked. Her ocean-blue eyes were gazing at him with concern and compassion. She wore a soft pink blouse, open at the neck and a short white skirt that showed off incredible legs.

She looked great. Classy, sexy. But he wasn't interested in women right now, classy or not. He figured his comment would make her leave him alone.

She looked a little taken aback, then laughed. "It didn't work. You've only made me curious. Why don't you let me buy you a cup of coffee?"

He shifted his crutches to a more comfortable position and resigned himself to the inevitable. "Make it a Scotch on the rocks and you're on."

"You shouldn't mix alcohol and pain meds."

"I'm not on any medication." He'd taken himself off the drugs and didn't mean to go back. He didn't like feeling dependent on the pills. And he didn't like the temptation of having them so handy. Whenever the pain was really bad, he took over-the-counter painkillers.

"All right. Where do you want to go? Do you have your car?"

He shook his head. What car? His truck was gone

and his own insurance company was dragging its heels on paying up. He could use his pitifully small savings for a down payment. Or some of the proceeds from the sale of his boat. Assuming it sold. He pushed that thought away.

"I took a cab." Because he didn't want to have to ask his family to drive him again. He was sick of asking them for help. They didn't begrudge it at all, but a man had some pride. Even if that's all he had.

"I want to go anywhere they don't know me."

"Meaning nowhere in Aransas City. Got it," she said, and started walking.

He followed her out to the parking lot on his crutches. Slowly. When they came to some stairs she detoured and took the ramp. "I can handle stairs," he said.

"I'm sure you can. But there's no reason to if you don't have to."

They reached her Porsche. With a pang he thought about his truck. A sweet black beauty that really hummed. *Had* hummed, he reminded himself.

"Let me move the seat back. I think you can fit."

Having no choice, he let her. Then he eased himself in. It took a while and he didn't like her seeing him struggle, but again, he had no choice. She didn't comment, just took his crutches once he was settled and stuffed them in the back before going around to the driver's side and getting in.

"When will you be able to drive again?"

"I could drive now. An automatic, anyway." His left leg would have to get a whole lot more mobile before he could drive a stick again. "Doesn't much matter. My truck was totaled in the wreck."

"I remember. I'm sorry."

He shrugged and looked out the window, then back at her. Her profile was as classic as the rest of her. Man, she was some gorgeous woman. What was she doing with him? "Why are you doing this?"

She glanced at him, then turned back to the road. "Doing what? Having a drink with an attractive man?"

He snorted. "A man who can't walk without crutches. Who may never be able to walk worth a damn again." He thought, but didn't add, A man who was going to be flat broke in a matter of months.

"With that attitude you won't."

So she was a hard-ass. Oddly enough, that cheered him up. He liked that about her. "You wouldn't go out with me before," he reminded her. "I don't need a mercy date."

"We're having a drink," she said mildly. "I wouldn't call it a date."

"You don't need to call it a date, for it to be a date." He repeated the words she'd used at Gail's party. Then let the subject drop. He didn't really care why she was going as long as she took him somewhere he could get a drink. "Why did you come to Aransas City? You're obviously a city girl."

"I had my reasons."

"Such as."

"Private reasons. How does this look?" she asked, pulling up in front of a place that was sparkly, shiny new, with lots of glass windows and plants everywhere.

Too rich for his blood. But he didn't say that. "Looks fine." What the hell, it wasn't every day you found out you were soon to be broke and jobless.

She had to help him get out. There was no possible way he could make it out of that low-slung car on his own. He gritted his teeth and let her pull him up, hating the humiliation of needing assistance, hating that it hurt like hell just to get out of the car.

She was stronger than she looked, which was good considering he pushed one-eighty. Or he had before the wreck. He'd lost weight, and it didn't look good on him.

She got out his crutches and handed them to him. "Gabe, it's not a big deal."

"Maybe not to you."

They found a table in the corner where he was able to sit on the soft bench and stretch out his leg. It ached like crazy, not a surprise considering he'd been on his feet all day, and he massaged it surreptitiously. Lana ordered a glass of white wine and he ordered Scotch on the rocks.

"And keep it coming," he told the waitress.

Lana took a sip of wine and watched him down half his drink. "Do you want to talk about it?"

"Yeah, that's just what I like to do with a beautiful woman. Talk about how miserable my life is."

"You're alive. As I recall, that was in doubt for a while."

Yeah, he was alive. Big deal. "Is this where I'm supposed to thank you for saving my life?"

"I didn't save your life. The EMS team and emergency room doctors did that. I just called for help." She sipped wine.

"You got the license number of the truck that hit me." Which he'd yet to thank her for. "Thanks."

She just nodded and took another sip of wine. "What happened with your doctor that upset you so much?"

"Why do you care? You hardly even know me." He knew he sounded surly, but he didn't much care.

"True, but I know a lot of people who know you. Who care about you, so I assume they can't all be wrong. You're my partner's brother-in-law. Jay cares about you. He's a friend of mine."

At least she wouldn't mouth platitudes at him and try to paint a rosy picture like his sisters insisted on doing. His brother Cam didn't say much at all, not being a very good liar. Neither of his brothers-in-law said much, either. Mostly because he avoided them whenever possible. Like he wanted to avoid everyone he knew.

"I just got the death knell on my job."

"Your charter fishing service?"

"Yeah. It's going to take longer than I thought for

me to get back to work. I can't afford to let my boat sit idle."

"So what are you going to do?"

"Sell it." God, it hurt to say that. Hurt to even think it. He loved his boat. Loved his work.

"How long does Dr. Black expect your recovery to take?"

"He didn't want to commit, but his best guess was two years for a full recovery. Or more." Gabe shook his head and knocked back another dose of forgetfulness.

"And you can't afford to keep your boat until you recover."

"Nope."

She was quiet a moment, then said, "Well, that blows."

He laughed. For the first time in three months he found something amusing. "Yeah, it sure does."

"You love your job, don't you?"

He thought about it. Something he'd tried really hard not to do in the past three months. "Sometimes, in the middle of summer, you go out to the blue water and it's so still you almost can't catch your breath. Not a breeze stirring, nothing but you and that hot, still air and rolling blue water. That's what they call the deep water where the big fish are. Blue water."

She was looking at him now, and he could see she was really interested in what he was saying. "The sky's blue, too, not a cloud in it, so clear you can't see anything but blue forever, and so damn bright it hurts your eyes. You run, trolling the bait behind you, watching the flying fish skip over the waves and the gulls circle overhead, looking down in the water for signs of the big ones, the marlin and sail. If you're lucky, really lucky, you'll hook one."

She leaned forward, her eyes intent on his. "What happens then?"

"They light up so bright that their colors are incandescent. All shades of blue, sometimes green, yellow. Neon rainbow colors. And they dance. They fly out of that water and tail walk on the waves. They leap like you've never seen anything do. They're so amazing, sometimes you don't even mind when they throw the hook."

"It sounds incredible."

He laughed. "It can be. Of course, I haven't told you about all the times you go out and hook nothing but dry eyes and sunburn."

"No, but I thought fishermen always talk about the ones that got away."

She was smiling. Man, she had some beautiful eyes. "Your eyes," he said.

"What about my eyes?"

"They're blue-water eyes. Fathoms deep, just like that blue water."

"Now that's a line I've never heard before." She laughed, but looked pleased. "I had no idea you were a poet."

"Just call me Will." For a minute he'd almost felt normal again. Flirting with a pretty woman, talking about fishing. Other than sex, what more could a man ask for?

Then he remembered. He wouldn't be fishing again. Not for years, if ever again. He picked up his drink and chugged some.

"So what are you going to do?"

Lana was no dummy. She'd seen the minute his mood had changed. "I don't know." He drained his glass and signaled the waitress. "Fishing's all I've ever done. If I can't fish…" He closed his eyes and shook his head. "I don't know how I'm going to make a living."

"There must be something else you're interested in. Something else you can do. At least until you recover and can think about fishing again."

"Besides flipping burgers, I don't know what." He shrugged. "Who'd want to hire a thirty-eight-year-old man with a bad leg who's never done anything but fish?" Oh, he'd held other jobs, of course, quite a few. But nothing he'd want to make a career of.

"What about your brother? Maybe he could use some help with the restaurant."

"I'm not taking charity from my brother. Or any of the rest of my family, either."

She took another sip of wine and considered him. "Do you remember anything about the accident?"

"Not much. I remember you talking to me afterward." And he remembered the pain. The misery of those first weeks made what he endured now seem like a picnic.

"You were in bad shape. You almost bled out. Some people would say you're lucky to be alive."

He took the refill from the waitress and knocked some back. "Some people aren't thirty-eight years old with no visible means of support."

"Why don't you try to do something positive, like figure out what else you'd like to do for a living?"

"Because I can't think of anything, that's why. I'm a fisherman. That's it."

"I understand you're upset. Anyone would be. God knows, you have reason. But sooner or later, you have to accept what life deals you. Sooner is better."

They'd been getting along fine until she had to remind him of reality. "You're just full of good advice, aren't you, Dr. Do-Good?"

"You don't have a corner on pain and suffering."

The quiet statement set his anger off like a torch. "What do you know about pain? You sit in that clinic and hand out lollipops to kids and tell your adult patients to take two aspirin and go to the emergency room."

She paled. "You're wrong. I know a lot about pain." She leaned forward and captured his gaze. When she spoke, her voice was low, but he heard every word. "I know what it's like to want to slap the next well-meaning person who gives you a pitying look and then looks away because he or she doesn't know what to say. I know what it's like to drink yourself into oblivion, hoping, praying, you'll forget. But you can't. There's not enough liquor in the world to drown that pain."

He started to speak but she held up a hand and continued, her eyes fierce, holding a deep sorrow. "I know what it's like to look at a bottle of pills and think about how damn easy it would be to take them all and escape that way." She looked away, picked up her glass and drank another sip. "Trust me, I know. Better than you do."

Well, hell. He was an idiot. "I'm sorry," he said gruffly. "When I screw up, I don't do it halfway. What happened?"

Expressionless, she looked at him for a long moment. "None of your business."

CHAPTER THREE

"I'M SORRY," he said again.

Horrified, she stared at him. "No, I'm sorry. I had no right to go off on you that way." She could have kicked herself. She never did that, never lost control so easily. The poor guy had just been dealt a major blow, and here she was ripping his face off because of an unthinking comment he'd made. He didn't deserve that. No one did.

"Sure you did. And you were right. I've been sitting around feeling sorry for myself and it's not doing anyone a damn bit of good. Least of all me."

"I shouldn't have said what I did. I'm not usually that insensitive. But you…you pushed a button."

"I might be stupid, but I'm bright enough to figure that out."

"I don't think you're stupid at all." He was a lot more perceptive than she'd imagined when she'd first met him. "Gabe." She touched his hand, then covered it with hers. "You had an accident that altered your life. It takes time to come to terms with that. It's natural to want things back the way they were before...that life-changing event."

"How long did it take you?"

She opted for honesty. "I still deal with it every day. I'm not sure I'll ever come to terms with it completely."

"That's comforting."

"Would you rather I lied?"

His mouth twisted into a wry grin. "Absolutely." He looked down at the table, where her hand still covered his. Turned his hand over so they were palm-to-palm and looked into her eyes. "And I'd a hell of a lot rather you had a different reason for holding my hand."

His eyes were brown. A warm, dark chocolate, rich and tempting. If only she were young again. Carefree. Whole. Maybe...if she pretended hard enough she could believe that life could be simple again. That she was a normal woman, doing all the normal things women did. Things like dating. Things like... No, even she couldn't pretend that much.

"What are you thinking?" he asked softly.

She wanted to help him. Wanted him to be able to enjoy life fully again. Maybe she could get him started. It meant taking a risk, but if she spelled out the terms, then it would work. "I'm thinking of taking you up on that offer."

He blinked. Taking advantage of his momentary distraction, she slipped her hand out of his. She took a deep breath and a sip of wine.

"What offer?"

"The night we met. You offered to take me fishing."

His expression turned sour. "That isn't going to happen. I can't handle my boat. Which you ought to know since I've been crying in my beer about having to sell it." He picked up his drink and downed some.

"Why do we have to use your boat?" He looked at her and she could see that idea had never occurred to him. "I see people fishing from the piers all the time." She didn't pause to consider how reckless she was being. She wasn't thinking of herself and her rules. She was thinking of him and the sorrow and pain that lurked in his eyes, except when he talked about fishing.

Or flirted with her. And that was a very heady feeling. Heady…and terrifying at the same time.

"Gabe?"

He smiled, a slow, sexy curve of his lips. "I thought you didn't date. That definitely sounds like a date."

"It's not a date," she said quickly. She'd tried dating after her divorce. But it had been a disaster. Dating led to expectations she couldn't fulfill. Not after what had happened to her. So she had to tell Gabe up front she wasn't interested in him that way. Except, if she were honest with herself, she knew she could be.

He didn't comment, just raised his eyebrows and looked at her.

"I'm talking about two friends going fishing and having fun. Not a date at all. Are you up for that?"

He smiled again and she wasn't sure he believed her, but he only said, "You're on."

GABE CALLED Lana a couple of days later. "Hey, it's Gabe. Change of plans about Saturday," he said. He shifted, trying to get comfortable on his couch.

"You can't go," she said.

She sounded relieved, which annoyed him. "You think I'm calling to cancel?"

"Aren't you?"

"Nope. I have a truck now, so I can pick you up." The insurance had finally paid and he'd bought a used truck. It was ugly, but it ran and it had automatic transmission. Most important, it had been cheap.

Silence. Then, "Gabe, maybe we shouldn't—"

Not wanting to hear some lame excuse, he interrupted. "Yeah, forget it. I get the picture," he said, and hung up.

The phone rang a minute later. He thought about not answering, but shrugged and picked up. "What?"

"Do you always jump to conclusions like that?" Lana asked.

"Why waste time? You changed your mind. Big deal." But it was to him, which made him pretty damn pathetic.

"I did not change my mind. Exactly. But I…I

started thinking afterward and I wondered if it was a mistake for us to go fishing."

"Why would it be a mistake?" Then it dawned on him. "Oh, like rubbing salt in my wounds."

"Yes."

Plausible, but he wasn't sure that was all of her reason. Or even if it was the truth. One way to find out, though. "Do you want to go fishing or not?"

"Well...yes."

"Then we'll go. I'll pick you up around two and we'll grab a bite to eat afterward. Be sure to bring a hat and cover up your legs and arms, or else you'll fry."

"As long as you're sure. I don't want to push you into doing something you're not ready for."

Or was it something she wasn't ready for? He wondered if her ban on dating was connected to the tragedy in her past. "I wouldn't have agreed if I didn't want to do it. I'll pick you up Saturday at two."

"All right. Saturday, then."

The doorbell rang as he was hanging up. "It's open," he called.

His sister came in, carrying a bunch of papers. Business stuff, probably, since Cat was his accountant. His mood went downhill fast. She didn't look happy.

"Hi." She put the papers on his coffee table and started straightening things, stacking newspaper, moving objects around. She did that a lot, but especially when she was nervous. Or upset, and today she looked to be both. "Do you have some time to go over your accounts?"

He'd wanted to put off telling his family, but it looked as though he was out of luck there, too. "Let me guess, things look grim."

She sat beside him. "I'm sorry, Gabe."

He shrugged. "Know anybody who wants to buy a fishing boat?"

"It's not that bad. You should be able to get by until you can go back to work."

Yeah, if it wasn't going to be two years or more. "I'm selling *El Jugador*." She started to argue, but he held up a hand. "I'm selling the boat. That's my final decision. And I don't want to discuss it."

Because he knew if he told her the whole story, she'd try to talk him out of it. She'd offer to lend him money until he got back on his feet. She already had. All of his family had. And by God, he was not going to live on his family's charity.

Her eyes filled with tears. "Don't do that," he said. "You know I hate that."

"I can't help it. It's so unfair. You were doing great until—" She halted and sniffed, unwilling to finish the sentence, but Gabe finished it for her, silently.

Until the accident that ruined his leg…and his life. "Do me a favor and tell the rest of the family. Tell them I don't want to talk about it."

"Gabe, we want to help."

"You can't. Not anymore. I have a truck now, so I can get around. Just… You need to back off, Cat. All of you need to back off."

"We can't back off. We're your family. We love you and want to help."

He couldn't deal with them anymore. They were smothering him with love and concern. "Leave me alone, Cat. I'm fine. Go home."

He'd have told her not to come back but short of moving across country, he didn't see any way of enforcing that order. None of his family would accept it. The Randolphs stuck together.

He finally got her to leave, then he pulled a piece of paper out of his pocket and looked at the number he'd jotted down earlier. The sooner he made the call, the sooner he could quit thinking—no, obsessing—about having to do it. A clean knife straight to the heart.

He punched in the number. "Yeah, I want to take out a classified ad. For sale, 1991 Chris-Craft, 34-foot sport fisher…"

LANA CHANGED four times before she decided on what to wear. Khaki slacks and a pink T-shirt shouldn't have taken that long to pick, but she knew her indecision was a defense tactic to prevent her from calling off the date.

Not a date, she corrected herself. Just fishing,

with a friend. Nothing to worry about, right? Gabe had been cool with that. At least, he'd seemed to accept what she'd said.

And she wanted to help him. Wanted him to have fun. She wanted to have fun herself for a change.

It had nothing to do with the fact that Gabe evoked feelings in her that she hadn't experienced in a very long time. Feelings she didn't quite trust.

She picked up a lightweight, long-sleeved shirt to throw over the T-shirt, knowing there wasn't enough sunscreen in the world to keep her from burning. The doorbell rang and she went to the door and looked out the peephole. As she'd expected, it was Gabe. She unfastened the locks and opened the door. "Hi. I meant to be ready so you wouldn't have to get out of the car."

He wore faded jeans and a white, short-sleeved T-shirt with a picture of a fish on it that was just tight enough to hint at some serious muscles. Not surprising, considering the physical nature of his job. Obviously the effect of years of physical labor didn't disappear in a few months.

He leaned on his crutches and flashed her a smile. "I'm Southern. My mother would kill me if I sat in the car and waited for a woman to come out to me. Are you ready to go?"

"As soon as I set the alarm." She did that, then shut the door and locked up.

He lifted an eyebrow. "You have a burglar alarm? In Aransas City?"

"I'm the cautious sort," she said as they reached the truck. "Where are we going to eat?"

He opened her door, then went around to his side, tossed his crutches in the truck bed and got in. "I thought we'd go over to Corpus Christi. There's a good Mexican restaurant over there. How does that sound?"

"We're going all the way to Corpus? What's wrong with here?"

"It's not that far, not even half an hour away. I know everyone we're likely to see here and I don't want to talk to anybody."

"Not even your family?"

"Especially not my family."

He didn't sound angry, but he sounded definite. "Why are you upset with them?"

"I'm not. I'm just sick of them fussing over me. And now that they know I'm selling the boat, they're going to be even worse."

She wanted to tell him she was sorry about his boat, but given his comment, she didn't think he'd appreciate her sympathy. Instead she said, "I've met your brother Cameron and he doesn't seem the sort to fuss."

"He doesn't. Not really. The women fuss. Especially my mother. If I hadn't convinced her to go on a trip with her new husband, she'd still be at my house fussing over me. But Cam just..." He shrugged. "He wants to help and he can't. They all want to help and they can't and…" Again, he trailed off, drumming his fingers on the steering wheel.

"It's driving you crazy."

He glanced at her and smiled. "Yeah."

"You want them to treat you like they did before the accident and nobody does."

"Yeah," he said again. "How did you know?"

"Been there, done that," she said. And moved fifteen hundred miles across country to avoid it.

He was quiet a moment, digesting her comment. "Is that why you won't talk about what happened to you?"

"It's one of the reasons." But she had talked about it. To other survivors. And to her counselor, though that hadn't lasted long. Now she was done with talking. "So, have you had any ideas about what you're going to do?"

"Very subtle," he said as they pulled into the parking lot by the end of the pier.

It took them a while to get situated since Lana had to carry most of the gear. She could tell that bothered Gabe, but there was no way he could carry much when he was on crutches.

After they set up the folding chairs and arranged the rest of their stuff, he spoke again. "I haven't had any brilliant ideas about a job. It's going to have to be something flexible, since I'll probably be having more surgery."

"We don't have to talk about it, if you don't want to," she said.

"Might as well. Like I said, I've never thought about doing anything else but fishing. It's hard to wrap my mind around the fact that I don't have a choice." He reached in the bucket beside him and pulled out a shrimp. "You've fished before, right?"

"No, never."

His eyebrows raised. "You've really never been fishing at all? Never? How could you live on the California coast and never fish?"

"I don't know." She shrugged, feeling a little inadequate. "I grew up in the city, and my parents weren't big on the outdoors. After that, no one ever suggested it, so I never learned."

"Okay, first you're going to learn to bait the hook." He held the shrimp and put the hook through the shell on its back, behind its head. "Like that, see?" He let her look at it closely, then took the shrimp off and held the hook and the bait out to her.

She looked at the wiggling shrimp suspiciously. "Poor little guy. Why can't we use dead ones? I don't mind dead ones."

"Live is better. Come on. You try it."

Gingerly she took the shrimp from him and threaded it on the hook as he'd told her to. She listened intently while he explained what to do with the rod and reel. It didn't look too difficult. She pulled her arm back and let fly—behind her.

"Crud. This is harder than it looks." She reeled it

in and started over. This time she not only threw it behind her, she lost the bait. Fifteen minutes later, and frustrated beyond belief, she was no closer to success.

"Hold on." He picked up his crutches and got out of the folding chair. "Let me show you." He took the rod from her and demonstrated several times. She tried again and a few minutes later he was seated and unsnarling her line.

"Forget it," she said. "I'm a big, fat klutz."

"You're not a klutz. It's just something new for you." He got up again, balancing his bad leg on one crutch. "Come stand beside me here, so I can help you cast the line."

"You think I'm hopeless, don't you?"

"No, I don't think you're hopeless." She didn't move. "Lana, do you want to learn to fish or not?"

"Not."

He shot her an irritated glance.

"Oh, all right." She moved to his right side and he put his arm around her and put his hand over hers on the reel.

"Relax." He shook her arm. "The first thing you have to do is not stiffen up. No wonder you're having problems."

How could she relax when this was the closest she'd been to a man in ages? She tried to concentrate on what he was telling her and ignore the nerves jumping in her stomach.

"We'll just go through the motion first without

trying to cast." He pulled her arm back and guided it forward in a throwing motion, and after several tries, he let her cast the line into the water and reel it back in as he steadied her with his arm. She did that a number of times and then he said, "Now try it by yourself." He dropped his hand and moved away.

She hadn't wanted him to, she realized. Once her nerves had steadied, she'd enjoyed being near him. Maybe she wasn't as hopeless as she'd feared. Maybe she was finally ready to move on with her life. Concentrating, she did what they'd been practicing and her line went sailing, the bait landing in the water some distance away.

"I did it! Look, I did it!"

His smiled flashed. "You sure did. You're going to be a pro in no time."

"Now what?"

"You reel it in slowly and then do it again. Or you can leave it out there for a bit. You can sit down if you want," he said, and sat in his chair.

She reeled it in, cast again, then took her seat beside him and turned to look at him. "Why aren't you fishing?"

"Didn't want you to have to haul any more stuff than absolutely necessary."

"It's not a big deal, Gabe. Besides, I'm the one who conned you into bringing me. Maybe we should have waited until you were more mobile."

"Who knows when that will be. Although, I think

I'm going to be able to use a cane pretty soon." He gave her a wry smile. "Whoopee."

"You've made a lot of progress."

"That's what they tell me. You've got a bite," he said, motioning to her rod.

She felt something tugging on the line and saw the tip of the rod point down. "What do I do?" she asked.

"Reel him in." He laughed as she jumped up and turned the reel.

A few minutes later a huge fish flopped on the dock. "He's enormous! What is it? I can't believe I caught a fish that size." Feeling almost giddy, she laughed. Who knew fishing would be so fun? "I can't believe I caught one at all."

"Speckled trout. A couple of pounds, I'd guess. Good eating." He looked at her, smiling. He had a great smile, she thought. And dimples no grown man should have. "Keep him or throw him back?"

"If I keep it, will it still be good tomorrow?"

"Sure. We'll start a stringer. I'll filet your catch and that will keep in the cooler until we get back. But if you're not going to cook them tomorrow, you should freeze them when you get home."

"Keep it, then." She had an impulse to ask him to dinner, but she didn't follow it. That would be way too much like a date.

By late afternoon she'd added two more trout and a redfish to the stringer, besides catching an assortment of others they'd thrown back. They took the keepers to a wooden cleaning stand, and Gabe showed her how to filet them. After that they washed up and carried everything to the pickup, with Lana making two trips.

Gabe looked tired, she thought as they got in the truck, and wondered if the long afternoon had been too much for him. "We can go home if you want. We don't have to go to eat Mexican food."

He looked at her before starting the engine. "Aren't you hungry?"

"Yes, but… We could pick up fast food."

He tilted his head and considered her. "What are you trying to say that you're not saying?"

She sighed, knowing he wouldn't like admitting weakness. "You look tired. Is this your first long outing since your accident?"

"I'm fine, Lana."

"I don't want you to overdo it because of me."

"Are you sure that's what this is about? If you want to go home, just say so."

She pointed to his leg. "You've been rubbing your leg off and on for the last hour. I know it's hurting. If you're tired, we can skip the restaurant."

He frowned. "It won't hurt any less at home than it does here. Save the coddling for somebody else. I get plenty of that from my sisters and my mother."

"I'm not coddling you. I'm merely being practical. However macho you want to be, you're still recuperating."

"I'm not trying to be macho." She gave him a disbelieving look and he continued. "I forgot about it today. For the first time since the accident, I felt like myself again. I'm not ready for that to end yet."

Their eyes met and she smiled. "I'm not, either. Let's go eat." She understood, better than he knew. Because today was the first time in a very long time that she'd enjoyed the present and hadn't worried about the future. Even better, she hadn't thought of the past.

CHAPTER FOUR

"I'VE BEEN THINKING about your job situation," Lana said once they had their drinks. "Maybe you could go to school and study something you like."

Gabe choked on his iced tea. As tired as he was, if he'd gotten a beer, he'd have fallen asleep. "Me, go to school? You mean college?"

"Or graduate school. Yes, why not?"

"I'm thirty-eight years old, for one thing. And I don't have a college degree, so it would definitely be college." He laughed and shook his head. "Me in college. Yeah, that's going to happen."

"What's so funny about that?"

"Nothing, for someone like you. You're a doctor. You went to school forever, right?"

"Let's see, four years college, four years medical school, a year of internship, a two-year residency." She looked at him and nodded. "Yes, forever."

He grinned. "I hated school. Barely made it out of high school. I had two ambitions when I was in school. Three, if you count graduating. One was to fish and to make a living at it, which you know." He ate a couple of chips and drank some more iced tea.

"What was the other?"

"To get into Jennifer Whistlewhite's pants."

Lana choked. The waitress appeared with their food and set the steaming plates in front of them.

"You asked," Gabe said, preparing to dig in.

"True. Well, did you?"

"Unfortunately no." He ate some more and then continued. "She went steady with the captain of the football team and wouldn't give me the time of day." Jennifer Whistlewhite, his unrequited love all through high school. He hadn't thought about her in years.

"Although, she did go out with me once. To make her boyfriend jealous." He smiled reminiscently. What a dumb-ass he'd been.

"You didn't know."

He shook his head. "In those days I wasn't the brightest crayon in the box."

"Spoken like a man who's been burned."

More than once, he thought. "What about you?" he asked instead of answering. "Have you been burned?"

"I'm divorced." She gave him a wry smile. "What do you think?"

"Sorry. I forgot."

She didn't say anything and they ate in silence for a bit. She ate another bite, then laid her fork down and said casually, "It was another woman."

"What was another woman?"

"When I got burned. My husband had an affair."

"He left you for another woman?" He couldn't believe anyone would leave Lana for another woman, but then, it took all kinds.

She buttered a flour tortilla, then glanced up at him. Her face composed, her eyes a chilly, lake blue, she didn't look upset. She did that cool, calm and collected ice queen bit very well, he thought. Although she might not be quite so tranquil underneath it all.

"Yes. His therapist."

"Isn't that against the Hippocratic oath?"

She laughed and he had the satisfaction of seeing the chill leave her face. "It's unethical. I thought it was, anyway. But by then our marriage was all but over anyway. Frankly, I was…relieved."

"He sounds like a loser."

She started to say something, then shrugged. "He was."

"I'd like to think Jennifer was, too, but last I heard, she had a very successful modeling career."

She patted his arm consolingly. "Haven't you ever heard the expression 'what goes around comes around'?"

"Sure. But in my experience it never does. At least, not to the ones who deserve it."

"You're very cynical, aren't you?"

"Realistic," he corrected, and signaled for the check.

They walked to the truck in the gathering twilight.

He could feel the tension come over her like a storm cloud filling the sky. She seemed nervous, almost spooked, and she kept looking around as if she expected something to happen. When they'd first walked out she'd put her hand in her pocket. Now, as they approached the truck, she pulled something out of her pocket and held it clutched in her fist. A small canister, he realized.

"Lana, are you okay?" Gabe asked after they got in the truck.

"Of course. Why do you ask?"

He gestured at the pepper spray she still clutched in her hand. "Expecting trouble? Or did I say something to make you mad?"

She stared at it, then flushed. "Sorry. Habit." Hastily, she tucked it away.

Gabe didn't say anything. He simply started the truck and drove home. He might not be the most sensitive guy in the universe, but he was starting to get a pretty good idea of what might have happened in Lana's past. And if what he suspected was true, he needed to be very careful how he pursued her. Careful, and slow.

THE FOLLOWING afternoon Lana carted three flats of flowers out to her front yard. She'd had a devil of a time fitting them into the Porsche, but she'd finally managed. Dahlias and begonias, she had decided after much dithering. Exactly what her yard needed.

It was past time she did something about her dismal flower beds. The previous owner hadn't been much of a gardener, in fact, he'd hardly mowed the lawn. But Lana intended to get it in shape. Problem was, she knew zilch about gardening. She and Terence had lived in apartments their entire marriage. But she'd been studying, and the clerk at the lawn and garden store in Rockport, a small town to the north of Aransas City, had assured her she couldn't go wrong with what she'd chosen.

Her mind wandered as she planted the flowers, mostly thinking about yesterday and her date with Gabe. She had enjoyed it. Not just the fishing, but dinner afterward. She liked talking to Gabe. He was interesting, different from the men she used to date. And he was the polar opposite of Terence, an internist at the same hospital where she'd worked. Maybe that was part of his appeal.

After the divorce she'd gone on a few dates, but she hadn't wanted to get involved. Hadn't been able to deal with what dating invariably led to. She wasn't comfortable with physical intimacy, and the men she'd gone out with hadn't understood why. And why should they have, when she hadn't told them? Gabe, on the other hand, hadn't even tried to kiss her. Instead of being relieved, though, she'd been disappointed. She'd found herself thinking more and more about kissing him.

She wondered if he'd done it deliberately, so she'd

think about that. And him. And wonder. If so, he'd certainly accomplished his purpose.

"Nice flowers."

Startled, she looked up to see her neighbor, Maggie Barnes. She almost didn't recognize her without her police uniform. Today she wore white slacks and a sleeveless blouse, and her long red hair was down rather than pulled back in her usual ponytail.

"Hi, Maggie. Thanks."

They'd met when she moved in, then hadn't seen much of each other until the night of Gabe's accident. But while they waved at each other from a distance, Lana hadn't really gotten to know her.

"I'm a little early," Maggie said now. "You are going, aren't you?"

Lana looked up at her blankly. "Going where?"

"The party."

"What party?"

"The candle party."

Confused, Lana simply stared at her.

"You know, Sarah's candle party?"

"Sarah—" She got to her feet and shoved the hair out of her face before she remembered her hands were muddy. "Sarah Forester." Who was nice, but pushier than Lana was comfortable with. Which was why she hadn't committed to the party Maggie was talking about, and why she'd forgotten. Something about buying candles and playing games, Sarah had said. The whole idea hadn't appealed to Lana.

"She sent a police escort to be sure I'd come?"

Maggie let out a peal of laughter. "No, but please don't give her that idea. Sarah's my aunt."

"Oh, I'm sorry." Maggie laughed again and Lana winced. "Open mouth, insert foot. I meant, she's a very nice lady but I wasn't planning on going to the party."

Still smiling, Maggie nodded. "Which she obviously suspected since she asked me to bring you. Do you have other plans? Besides planting flowers?"

"Well…no. But I'm not exactly dressed for a party." She glanced at the flowers, realizing she'd planted all but a couple. No help there.

"Good. It saves time if we're honest. You don't want to come because it sounds boring and besides that, my aunt is the pushiest woman in three counties. Am I right?"

"Maybe not in three counties."

Maggie grinned. "Three, maybe even four. It's all right, I've known her all my life. And the candle party will almost certainly be every bit as boring as you're thinking. But it will make your life a lot easier if you just resign yourself to coming. Sarah won't nag you after that, but she has this obsession with making sure newcomers feel welcome. She's relentless until they come to at least one party."

Oh, what the hell. "When you put it that way, I guess I'd better come. Let me plant these last two and grab a shower. Will that make us too late?"

"Unfortunately not," Maggie said with a cheeky grin. "I'll be at my house waiting for you."

The party wasn't nearly as boring as Maggie had predicted. Lana enjoyed visiting with the women, several of whom were patients of hers. It was mostly an older crowd, with the exception of herself and Maggie. She also enjoyed Maggie's company, and her wicked, under-the-breath commentary on several of the ladies.

"You're dangerous," Lana told her when they got in the car to leave. "I almost bit my tongue when Letty Washburn played the piano for us and you told me she wanted to be a concert pianist." Poor Letty had been excruciatingly bad, not that anyone had seemed to mind, or even notice, for that matter.

"Sad, but true," Maggie said. "She's convinced if she hadn't married Harry and settled down here, she'd be as famous as Van Cliburn."

Lana's eyes widened as she choked back a laugh. "Oh, I'm glad you didn't tell me that then. I'd never have kept a straight face."

"The mind boggles," Maggie agreed. "Do you want to get some dinner? I think we deserve a reward after that party. We could go to the Scarlet Parrot."

"That sounds good." She had missed going out with her women friends, she thought. She'd had a few invitations from Gail, Jay's wife, and Gail's sister Cat, but for one reason or another, she hadn't been able to make many of them.

The Scarlet Parrot, Cameron Randolph's waterfront restaurant, was an inviting place with its dark-wood-planked floor and ceiling fans, the mounted fish on the walls and the TV above the bar invariably tuned to a sports show. Often the TV was muted and the jukebox could be heard, grating out country tunes. Or sometimes there was a live band, though the couple Lana had heard were terrible. Apparently Cam was too softhearted to turn anyone down, so often as not, the bands were lousy.

Cam's wife took their order herself. "I didn't realize you two knew each other," Delilah said, after bringing them their drinks.

"We're neighbors," Lana said.

"I dragged her to Sarah's party. And where were you? You were supposed to be there," Maggie said, lifting an eyebrow.

"Martha's on vacation," Delilah said. "So I couldn't leave Cam without any help."

"I might buy that, but Sarah won't," Maggie told her, taking a sip of iced tea.

"I'll avoid her for a week or so, until she forgets. Hopefully she won't hunt me down here. Say, Maggie, have you seen Gabe lately?"

"No. I take it you haven't, either."

Delilah shook her head. "I don't think he's been in more than three times since his accident."

Maggie scowled. "Probably holed up at home. He really needs to get out more. I bet he hasn't left his house in weeks unless it was to go to the doctor."

Lana cleared her throat. "He has at least once." They both looked at her inquiringly. "With me. Yesterday."

Both women stared at her. "You actually got him to go out?" Delilah asked. "How?"

"I asked him."

Delilah looked as though she wanted to say more, but a customer called her and she had to leave. Maggie drank some tea and eyed Lana speculatively. "So, you and Gabe."

"It wasn't a big deal. He took me fishing."

"How did he manage that?"

"Not on a boat." She sipped her drink. "We went to a pier."

"You're the first person who's convinced him to do anything fun—make that anything period—since the accident."

"Maybe I'm the first person who hasn't treated him like an invalid."

"You could have a point," Maggie acknowledged. "But it's hard not to when you see him on those crutches or remember the accident." She shuddered. "I hate car accidents. In a small town like this, they almost always involve people I know."

Delilah brought their food, but the restaurant was getting crowded so she couldn't stay to talk.

"So, you know everyone in town," Lana said.

"Sure. I've lived here most of my life. I spent a few years in Dallas, but then I came back."

"You didn't like the city?" Lana ate a piece of shrimp and sighed happily. Nothing was better than fresh seafood.

"Guess I'm just a small-town girl at heart," she said lightly, but some hidden undercurrent in her tone made Lana think there might be more to the story.

"What about you? What's a city girl from Los Angeles doing in Aransas City?"

"Making a new life," Lana said, surprising herself with her honesty.

Maggie didn't seem surprised. "This is a good place to start over. If you can stand the pace. Exciting it isn't."

"I like it." She was finally growing accustomed to the slower pace, and found she enjoyed not having to rush everywhere. Her patient load was lighter, as well, and without the trauma of the ER, her work was much less stressful.

Maggie shifted and looked uncomfortable. "Look, I know this is none of my business, but are you and Gabe—"

Lana interrupted. "I told you, it was no big deal. There is no 'me and Gabe.'"

Maggie studied her a moment, tapping her fingers on the table. "Would you like there to be?"

"I—don't know." It surprised her—and scared her—to realize that wasn't exactly the truth. She was interested all right, even though just the idea that she was attracted to a man again terrified her. But the fear warred with her desperate desire to be normal again. Would she ever be able to risk getting involved with someone?

Maggie ate a bite of food, then said, "Gabe's had it rough. He hasn't exactly been rolling in clover lately."

As Lana stared at the woman, an unexpected thought crossed her mind. "Are you warning me off, Maggie? Because if you're interested in Gabe, just tell—"

Maggie interrupted her, laughing. "Me and Gabe? No, it's nothing like that. I'm not sure the guy even realizes I'm female."

"I'm sure he does," Lana said dryly.

"If he does, he thinks about me like a sister. No, the reason I asked is… Well, it's like this. Gabe has the worst luck of anyone I've ever known."

"The accident, you mean."

"Not just that. A lot of things have happened, but they're not my business to tell you. Though if you listen to gossip you'll probably hear about them. Eventually, anyway."

She fell silent a moment, drumming her fingers lightly on the table, then looked at Lana again. "Gabe is snake bit. It seems like every time things start to go right for him, something goes wrong. Big time."

Like the accident and having to sell his boat, Lana thought. "And you don't want me to be one more thing that goes wrong in his life."

"Like I said, it's not my business. Just…be careful. He's a good guy."

"You're a good friend."

"That's me. Everybody's friend," Maggie said with a wry smile.

As she got ready for bed that night, Lana thought over the conversation about Gabe. He was snakebit, Maggie had said. Lana wondered what, besides the accident, had happened to him and if she'd ever find out. Her own luck hadn't exactly been stellar lately, either. Still, things had improved since she'd moved to Aransas City. Maybe both she and Gabe were due some good fortune for a change.

CHAPTER FIVE

"HEY, LANA, can you take the patient in exam one?" Jay asked her several days later.

"Take your patient? Why?"

"She fired me," he said, straight-faced. "She wants 'that new gal.'"

"What's the catch?" Lana asked suspiciously. Jay didn't ordinarily give away his patients. None of them did.

"No catch. Mrs. Lindstrom's a little hard of hearing," he said with a wink. "Nothing you can't handle, I'm sure."

I'm going to kill Jay, she thought half an hour later. Crotchety was about the kindest adjective she could think of for the woman. "Mrs. Lindstrom, you need to use your hearing aid," she shouted one more time. "Turn it on."

"Band-Aid? What do I need a Band-Aid for? Just here for my blood pressure checkup." The older woman scowled at Lana and added, "You're no better than that other young fella. Babies, that's what you are."

Lana gave up and wrote down what she wanted to tell her. Which didn't suit Mrs. Lindstrom, but Lana had run out of patience. After that she went to her office to finish up paperwork before lunch. Someone knocked on the door. "Come in," she called, thinking it was Bridget, the receptionist.

The door opened and her partner Tim's wife came in like a whirlwind. "Hope I didn't catch you at a bad time."

Lana closed the file on her desk and smiled. Tamara exuded energy, an interesting contrast to her more laid back husband. "No, I was just finishing up before lunch."

Tamara clasped her hands together and beamed. "Lana, you have to come to dinner Saturday night. Well, not just dinner, but a party. A small one, don't worry."

Immediately wary, Lana tried to think of an excuse. She liked Tamara, she really did, except for her habit of trying to pair off every single friend she and Tim had. Plus, a small party to Tamara could mean anything from two or three couples to half the town. "Oh, thanks for thinking of me, Tamara, but I really—"

"Don't say you can't." Green eyes beseeched her. "Tim ran into an old friend over in Corpus the other day and he's coming, too. I don't mind telling you, this guy is to die for. I know you two will hit it off."

"I can't. I have a date." The words were out before she could stop them. A lie, but she could not face being paired with a blind date. And though Lana had told her a number of times, Tamara simply didn't believe that Lana didn't date.

Tamara's face clouded for a minute, then she brightened. "Bring him, then. I'll find someone else for Allen. Maybe Maggie Barnes will come."

"Thanks, but I'm not sure what he was planning." Oh, Lord, she was digging herself in deeper with every word she spoke.

"Who is it?"

Lana stared at her blankly, and Tamara laughed. "Your date, who is it? Is it a secret?"

"No, of course not. It's…Gabe." *Please don't let Tamara have already asked him,* she prayed. *Just let me get out of this and I won't lie anymore, I promise.*

"Gabe Randolph?" Her face lit up. "Oh, that's perfect. I didn't realize you and Gabe were dating. We haven't seen him in ages, not since—"

Someone knocked and the partially open door behind Tamara swung wider. She knew it was Gabe almost before she saw him. Of course, who else would it be?

"Hey, Lana. Hey, Tamara. Sorry, didn't mean to interrupt. Bridget told me to come on back."

"Hi, Gabe. No, it's fine."

"Well, this is perfect," Tamara said brightly. "Lana and I were just talking about my party Saturday night. She wasn't sure what you'd planned but please tell me you'll both come."

"Saturday?" He raised an eyebrow and looked at Lana for an explanation.

"We'll talk it over, and I'll let you know, Tamara," Lana said hastily. Gently she ushered her out the door. "Thanks so much. I'll call you."

She shut the door and leaned her head back against it, closing her eyes. "Does she never give up?"

"Not when it comes to her parties. What's going on?" Gabe asked her.

"I'm not sure you want to know." She looked at him and smiled. "You're using a cane. That's wonderful."

He shrugged. "I wouldn't go that far, but it's better than crutches. I came by to see if you wanted to go to lunch."

"Lunch? Ah—Thanks, but—" She hesitated, not knowing what to say. If she went with him, he might think of it as a date. But she'd backed herself into a corner. She had to tell him about Tamara's party, otherwise she really would be up a creek. She was about to ask him for a big favor, maybe doing it over lunch would make it easier.

"I'm talking about grabbing a burger, Lana. You have to eat, don't you?"

"All right. But you may be sorry you asked after I tell you about my conversation with Tamara."

"No fear of that," he said, smiling.

He really did have a charming smile, she thought. Charming and just a bit dangerous. She couldn't quite figure out why she felt so comfortable and… safe with him. But she obviously did, because his had been the first—no, the only—name that had popped into her mind when she was looking for an excuse to avoid Tamara's matchmaking attempts.

"OKAY, so what's the deal with Tamara?" Gabe asked once they were seated in a booth at the tiny burger joint. It had only opened up a couple of weeks before, but he had already eaten here several times. The food was good and cheap. They had both ordered thick juicy hamburgers and crisp French fries, which were heaped on paper-lined plastic baskets on the table in front of them.

Lana took a bite and savored it before she spoke. "I lied to her. She was trying to set me up with a blind date for her party, and I said I had a date with you."

"Doesn't she know about your dating embargo?"

"Of course. I've told her at least ten times. She doesn't listen."

He took another bite and swallowed before speaking. "Do you want to go to the party?"

"I wouldn't mind. It's the blind date I object to."

So he was better than a blind date. Which, since he knew her opinion of blind dates, didn't do his ego much good. "Ever heard of just say no?"

She gave him a dirty look. "You know very well that doesn't work with Tamara."

"True." He set his burger down and smiled at her. "I guess this means you're going to have to go out with me. On a date." Could be worse, he thought philosophically. A date was a date, whatever the reason behind it.

"I—I guess it does. Do you mind? If you have other plans I'll just tell Tamara we can't come."

Mind? Did he mind going out with her? Those ocean blue eyes locked onto his and sucked him in. Apparently she didn't have a clue that he really liked her. Usually he didn't have trouble letting a woman know he was interested. But Lana was nothing like the women he used to date. B.A.—Before the Accident.

God, she looked pretty today. But then, every time he saw her, she looked great. And he was starting to think about her way too much for comfort.

What was up with him? She was just a woman. A beautiful one, but so what? What was it about Dr. Lana McCoy that made her stick in his mind? That made her different from every other woman he'd dated?

Well, for one thing, she wouldn't date. Except when forced into it.

Her eyes, which had been gazing at him anxiously, dropped. "I'm sorry to put you on the spot like this. Just forget it, I'll figure something out."

"Having a date with you isn't a hardship, Lana.

And no, I don't have plans." He picked up a fry and ate it. What would she say if they made it a real date and not a ploy to get out of a blind date?

"I sense a 'but' coming," Lana said.

"Does it have to be the party? We could do something else. Take in a movie in Corpus."

"No." Her response was quick in coming. Then she obviously realized how harsh she sounded. "I… I…told Tamara we would be there."

Well, he had his answer. "No you didn't. You told her we'd talk about it."

She glanced away, then asked, "Why don't you want to go to the party?"

"I didn't say I didn't want to go." But he didn't. For the same reason he didn't go to the Scarlet Parrot if he could help it. Because he was sick and tired of people treating him like an object of pity.

"You can't avoid everyone forever, you know."

"I'm not avoiding anyone." Which was a big, fat lie. He put down what was left of his burger and looked at her. "You really want to go, don't you?"

"It could be fun," she said a little wistfully. "I don't know that many people here yet, and I thought it would be nice to meet some more. But if you're that set against it, we can just forget the whole thing."

"We can go." It sounded like torture to him, but if it was the only way he could be with her, he'd do it.

"Are you sure?"

"I said we'd go, didn't I?"

She rewarded him with a blinding smile. "Thank you. You're very sweet."

He blinked, befuddled by her smile. "Sweet?"

She laughed. "Don't look so horrified. Hasn't anyone ever called you sweet before?"

He shook his head. "You're the first." Sweet, for God's sake. "I've been called a lot of things by women, but sweet isn't one of them."

She put her hand over his and gave it a light squeeze. "They were wrong. I think you're very sweet."

Oh, shit, he thought, gazing into those blue-water eyes of hers. It hit him like a marlin striking a twenty-pound test line, fast, hard and deadly. The reason he couldn't forget her, the reason he liked her so much. He was falling for her. Just steps away from being sucked under and dragged out to sea.

He should tell her to forget it. Cancel the date, stop seeing her, stop being friends. Now. Before he became any more involved. Because the very last thing he needed was to fall for—really fall for—a beautiful woman again and get slammed in the teeth. He'd done that once. No way, no how, was he doing it again.

He opened his mouth to tell her he'd changed his mind. "What time should I pick you up?"

CAM WAS WAITING on the front porch when Gabe got home. The familiar flash of guilt assailed him because he'd been dodging his brother just as he'd been dodging everyone else he knew. He got out of the truck and slowly made his way to the door, aware that Cam was watching him.

"When did you start using a cane?" Cam asked.

"A few days ago. It's not pretty, and I'm slower than a tortoise, but it's better than crutches." He opened the door and Cam followed him inside. "So, what's up?"

"Have I done something to piss you off?"

Gabe tossed his keys down, then went to sit on the couch and stare at his brother. "No, why would you think that?"

"Because you never come to the Parrot anymore. I can't remember the last time you came over."

He stretched his leg out and grimaced as he rubbed it. "Look, I'm just not feeling sociable, okay?"

"I think there's more to it." Cam sat in the overstuffed chair beside the couch and pinned him with a sharp glare. "And I have orders not to leave until I find out what the problem is."

Orders from Delilah, he'd bet. Women. Gabe rolled his eyes. "It's not my job to get your wife off your back."

"This is between you and me. Delilah has nothing to do with it."

Gabe simply lifted an eyebrow.

Cam grinned. "Okay, she has been on my case to

come see you. Delilah cares about you, too. So, why don't you make it easy on all of us and just tell me what's going on."

Maybe he should. It might clear the air. "What the hell. You won't let me pay for anything when I come to the restaurant. So I figured I wouldn't come in."

Cam just looked at him, as if waiting for more. After a moment he said, "That's it? That's your reason?"

"Yeah." He scowled at his brother. "I don't like feeling like a charity case. I can afford to buy my own damn food and drinks."

"Well, hell, why didn't you just say so?"

"I did. You weren't listening." None of his family listened. They just kept on offering, kept on trying to help.

"I didn't mean to—"

"Yeah, I know," Gabe interrupted. None of them meant to hurt him. They just didn't get it. "Forget it."

"Okay, no more freebies. Are we square now? You'll start coming in again?"

"Yeah." Even though he still didn't feel like being sociable, he'd make the effort. "Is that the only reason you came over?"

"No." Cam smiled and pulled a couple of cigars out of his pocket, handing Gabe one.

Gabe looked at the cigar, then at his brother, who was grinning like the Cheshire cat. "Let me guess, Delilah's pregnant."

"She is." Cam struck a match and held it out for Gabe to light his cigar. "She sure is. And due in a little less than seven months." He lit his own cigar and leaned back, still smiling.

"Congratulations," Gabe said, and put out his hand to shake his brother's. "So, how does it feel, Pop?"

Cam shook his head. "Still kind of hard to believe. I figured I'd never have kids, you know?" He laughed and added, "Of course, I never thought I'd be married, either. Until I met Delilah. Now I can't imagine not being with her."

"Yeah, funny how things work out." At first Gabe'd thought Delilah was bad news, but he'd been wrong. He'd never seen his brother as happy as he'd been ever since he'd met and married her. "How's Delilah? She doing that pregnancy hormone thing Gail and Cat did?"

"Not too bad so far. She hasn't had much morning sickness, either." Cam puffed on his cigar then looked at Gabe. "It's great. I mean, we were trying to get pregnant, so it's not like it was a surprise. But now that it's happened—"

He got up to search for an ashtray and came back with it a moment later. He sat again, stubbed out his cigar and blew out a breath. "If you want the truth, it's a little terrifying. I mean, I'm going to be a father."

"Yeah, so? It's not like you haven't ever been

around kids. We've got five nieces and nephews, for crying out loud. You see them all the time."

"It's not the same," Cam insisted. "What if I screw up? I'm responsible for this baby. I don't know anything about being a father."

"You have a wife," Gabe pointed out. "You don't have to raise the kid alone." He waited a minute and added, "I don't think I've ever seen you this neurotic. Are you going to be like this for the next seven months?"

Cam laughed. "I hope not. But it's a lot to take in. I guess being neurotic goes with the territory." He looked at his watch. "I'd better get going soon. But first I want to warn you, you'll be hearing from Gail and Cat soon. And probably Delilah, too."

"Why?"

He got up and grinned down at Gabe. "Tamara Kramer's been burning up the phone lines."

"Crap."

"So, you and the lady doc, huh? Your taste is improving. This one's not only beautiful, she even has a brain."

Gabe scowled at him. Damn small towns and all talkative women. "It's no big deal. Lana and I are friends, that's all."

Cam laughed. "Right. I believe that."

"It's true."

"You're serious." He stared at him a moment. "Is that all you want?"

Gabe half laughed. "What do you think?"

"Good, you had me worried for a minute there."

"I had a hard enough time just getting her to be friends. She won't even date."

"You're taking her to the Kramers' party. That's a date," Cam pointed out.

It went against the grain to admit it, but Cam was his brother, after all. "Only because she wanted to get out of being set up with a blind date." He shrugged. "Not because she really wants to go out with me."

"You're underrating yourself, Gabe. Nobody's forcing her. She must see something she likes in you."

"Maybe," he said, cheering up a little. Good point, he thought.

"Why doesn't she date?"

"She hasn't told me. But I have a feeling I know." Because some scum had assaulted her, he'd bet. Maybe someone she'd dated. It was the scenario that best fit her behavior.

"I'd better get going. The dinner rush is going to start soon." He walked to the door then turned to look back at Gabe. "You really like her, don't you?"

He shrugged again. "She's okay."

Cam laughed and went out the door.

For a long time after Cam left, Gabe sat and thought. He was pleased for his brother. After the hell they'd gone through, Cam and Delilah deserved to be happy and he was glad they were. But he was also, he was disgusted to discover, jealous.

Not that he had any interest in a wife and kids and for himself, but sometimes he wondered what it would be like to be that crazy about a woman and have her feel the same way about him.

The only woman he'd ever been totally gone over had taken him for the biggest ride of his life. And he sure as hell wasn't anxious to repeat the experience.

CHAPTER SIX

SATURDAY MORNING the phone rang while Gabe was lifting weights. His physical therapist had told him it was important to keep his entire body in shape, not just build up his leg, so he'd scrounged a bench and some free weights from a friend who wasn't using them. He'd never had to worry about being fit before. It had come naturally with his job.

The phone continued to ring and he remembered the ad he'd taken out. Damn, he didn't like the phone at the best of times and now he'd have to talk to every joker who called, no matter whether they were serious buyers or not. Groaning, he replaced the bar and went to answer it.

An hour and a half later, he'd finished showing the boat and was waiting for the buyer, Bart Stephens, to do something other than stare at *El Jugador* and scratch his head. He hadn't seemed too impressed, so Gabe couldn't figure out what he was still doing here.

"All right," Stephens finally said. "I'll make you

an offer." He named a price that was thirty thousand under the asking price. An asking price that was already low.

Gabe couldn't believe it. The guy, a wizened man of about sixty-five, was looking at him as though he expected Gabe to jump up and down over the offer. "Don't waste my time," he said, and limped away.

"Hey, I'm serious."

Gabe stopped and stared at him. "That price is a joke and you know it."

"Well—" He glanced at the boat, then back at Gabe. "I can give you two thousand more. But that's my final offer."

"Get lost," Gabe said, and left.

His bad mood lasted all day and was still there when he went to pick up Lana that night. As usual, she looked great. She wore another one of those short skirts she favored, this one in fire-engine red, and a sleeveless white blouse. Those blue eyes sparkled and her lips curved in a welcoming smile so pretty it actually made him ache.

Then he remembered she was only with him because she *didn't* want to go out on a blind date. Not because she wanted to be with him. Well, he'd known that when he'd agreed to take her. Why get bent out of shape over it now?

Because, dammit, he liked her.

"Gabe, is something wrong?"

"No, nothing."

"Then why are you scowling at me?"

"I wasn't." He turned away, limped down her front steps and opened the truck door for her.

The party was even worse than he'd imagined. He felt uncomfortable, out of sync, in a way he never had before the accident. He'd always been pretty sociable. You had to like people if you were going to run a successful charter boat service and in the past he'd enjoyed parties and being around others. But all that had changed the night of the accident. Now he just wanted to be left alone.

Which wasn't happening at this party. He couldn't move without someone offering him a chair and asking solicitously about his health. The fourth time it happened he managed a short thanks and escaped to the backyard while Lana was talking to a couple of other guests. Maybe if he sat, everyone would shut the hell up.

He took a sip of his beer and watched Lana deep in conversation. He shouldn't have come. But how could he turn her down when she'd looked so...wistful? Besides, he'd been too tempted by the thought of being with her to pay attention to his instincts. *Never ignore your gut,* he reminded himself now. *When you do, you deserve what you get.* He settled back to wait. It was going to be a long night.

"DO YOU WANT something to drink?" Lana asked Gabe later in the evening. "I'll go get you another beer if you want." They were sitting outside at a table in the Kramers' backyard, alone for the moment.

"No, thanks. I've still got some."

He didn't say anything else, which by this point in the evening didn't surprise her. He'd hardly spoken since he'd picked her up a couple of hours before. Lana was enjoying the party but she had a pretty good idea Gabe wasn't. She couldn't blame him. She'd heard all the anxious inquiries about his health. It had to be annoying to be treated as if you were going to fall over any moment.

Finally he'd gone outside and found a table. There he'd sat and nursed a beer the rest of the evening. People had stopped and visited with him but no one stayed long. Conversation was difficult with someone who spoke in one or two word sentences.

Well, what had she expected? He'd made it pretty obvious he hadn't really wanted to come. "Do you want to leave?"

He glanced at her, showing more animation than he had all night. "Why? Do you?"

She got up. "We might as well. You haven't said more than two words all night." He'd come as a favor to her, so she had no right to be annoyed, but she was.

"Lana? Is it really you?"

Lana turned to the man standing beside her. "Allen? What are you doing here?"

"Tim's an old friend of mine. I would have been here earlier but I was held up. It's great to see you."

He smiled and hugged her, all blond good looks and killer charm. "I moved to Corpus Christi. And apparently, you've moved, too. Tell me, how is Terence? How did you get him to move? I always thought he was fixed in L.A."

Uncomfortable, she extricated herself—not too obviously, she hoped. "As far as I know, he's still in L.A. We're divorced." A few years earlier, Allen Paxton had worked with her ex-husband in L.A. before moving away. But she hadn't known where.

"Oh, I'm sorry. I had no idea." He smiled ruefully. "Must be in the air. I'm divorced, too."

She glanced at Gabe, who was watching them with an expression she couldn't read. "Gabe, this is Allen Paxton. Allen, Gabe Randolph."

The two men shook hands and exchanged greetings. Then Allen turned back to her. "How about dinner? We can catch up on old times. Are you busy tomorrow?"

She glanced at Gabe who was smiling at her now, but rather cynically. "I, uh, thanks, Allen, but I can't."

He looked from Gabe to her, then back at her. "Sorry, I didn't realize you were here with a date. I guess it wouldn't do any good to ask if you're free another night?"

Her eyes met Gabe's for a long moment. "You guessed right," he said. He reached for her hand and held it, still looking at her with that faint, cynical smile. "She's taken."

Allen lifted an eyebrow. "I see. Well, it was good to see you again, Lana. Randolph, nice to meet you." He nodded at Gabe and walked off.

She blew out a breath, then pulled her hand from Gabe's and frowned at him. "Taken? Taken?" she repeated. "What am I, a parking space?"

"Don't complain." He smiled at her sardonically. "You're lucky I said anything at all. I could have let you squirm out of it by yourself."

She stared at him a moment. "You're mad."

He took a sip of beer and slapped the can down. His dark eyes were heated and flashing with annoyance. "Yeah, Lana, I'm mad."

"I didn't ask you—"

"Please," he said, clearly growing more irritated by the minute. "You gave me that wounded doe look. What was I supposed to do?"

Wounded doe? Had she really looked like that? Surely not. "I'm perfectly capable of turning down a date without any help from you."

"Is that so? Then why did you tell Tamara you had a date with me tonight?"

He had her there. And it took the wind completely out of her sails. She sat. "You're right. I'm sorry."

His jaw tightened as he gave her a long look. "Forget it. No big deal." He picked up his beer again and sipped it.

It dawned on her that he wasn't simply angry. He

was hurt. And she was a jerk. "Gabe, getting out of a blind date wasn't the only reason I asked you to bring me to Tamara's party tonight."

He shot her a derisive glance. "Yeah, right. Tell that to someone more gullible."

"Do you think I'd ask you to come with me if I didn't enjoy being with you?"

"You tell me."

"All right, I will. I had fun when we went fishing. I like being with you. Even if Tamara hadn't tried to set me up, I would have wanted to go out with you again."

Clearly unconvinced, he didn't say anything. He just looked at her with that faintly mocking smile curving his mouth.

"You don't believe me, do you?"

He shook his head. "Nope."

"You think the only reason I asked you to come with me tonight was to get out of the blind date."

"Yep."

She was horribly, guiltily aware he was right. She probably wouldn't have gone out with him again if she hadn't lied to Tamara and been forced into it. She'd been using him and he'd called her on it. The fact that she'd asked him because she felt safe with him didn't make it right.

And now she'd gone and used him again, to get out of the situation with Allen. Talk about adding insult to injury. The least she could do was own up to it. "I'm sorry. I shouldn't have done that. It was...not very nice of me."

"Like I said, forget it."

But she couldn't. She'd hurt his feelings and he didn't deserve that. Not after he'd been so nice to her. "What can I do to make it up to you?" she asked.

He looked at her speculatively, his gaze lingering on her mouth. Oh, God, was he going to kiss her? Or expect her to kiss him? Part of her wanted to. The other part thought it was a really bad idea.

Because kissing could lead to other expectations. And while kissing was one thing, she knew she wasn't ready for anything more.

"Come out with me," he said. "On a real date. To the Scarlet Parrot for dinner tomorrow night."

If she didn't go, it would kill any hope of friendship between them. Not to mention the possibility for anything more. Besides, if she were honest, she'd have to admit she wanted to go with him.

"All right. I'll have dinner with you."

He didn't smile but he searched her eyes. "Are you going out with me because you want to or because you feel like you have to?"

She put her hand over his where it rested on the table. "Because I want to."

This time he did smile. "Good."

Her stomach fluttered. All he'd done was smile at her, and her stomach was dancing with nerves. Oh, Lord, she was in trouble.

GABE WAS SURPRISED Lana had agreed to the date. In fact he'd almost expected her to back out, but when he didn't get a call, he showed up at her house Sunday night. He rang the bell and waited. After a bit he rang it again. Still, she didn't answer. Great, she'd stood him up. What a fool he'd been to think she was any different than any other woman.

He'd made it down the steps to the sidewalk when he heard the door open and she called his name. He turned around and looked at her.

"Gabe, I'm sorry. I heard the bell but I couldn't get away. I could use some help. Please hurry."

He climbed the steps again and followed her inside. "What happened to you?" She wore linen slacks and a sleeveless blouse but both were soaking wet. The clothes clung to her like a second skin, outlining generous breasts and a beautifully curved body. He tried to reroute his gaze from her body to her face but it was damn hard to do.

"I had the bright idea to throw a load of clothes in before we left," she told him as they walked to the kitchen. She opened the door to the laundry room and waved a hand at a disaster. Water was squirting out from behind the washer and already pooling on the floor. No wonder she was soaked.

"My washer has lost its mind."

"That's one way of putting it," he said, amused. He waded in, moving carefully because he didn't want his cane to slip, and reached behind the washer to turn off the water, getting his own shirt soaked in the process. "The hose broke," he said. "Got a spare? I can fix it if you do."

"Not unless the previous owner left one. And since the only things I've found that they left behind were dried-out paint cans, I doubt it. I don't imagine any store that carries things like that will be open on a Sunday night, either."

"Probably not. I can fix it for you tomorrow after work if you want me to."

"I can just call the repairman. But thanks, it's sweet of you to offer."

"There's no need to pay someone else to do something I can do for you in five minutes for free."

Willing to argue, he turned around to look at her and nearly groaned. She'd gotten down on her hands and knees and begun mopping up the water with towels.

Gabe abandoned any attempt to stop looking. She had the finest—

"Are you sure you don't mind?" She continued pushing the towel around.

"Mind what?" he repeated blankly.

"Gabe!"

He switched his gaze to her face. "What?"

"Are you staring at my butt?"

"Uh—" He decided she'd know if he lied so he shrugged and admitted it. "Yeah." He grinned. "It's kind of impossible not to with you in that position."

She sat back on her heels and frowned at him, but

then her lips twitched and he figured she wasn't really mad. "That's so…so—"

She stopped, apparently at a loss for words, so he finished for her. "Hey, I'm a guy. And you have to know you're one beautiful woman."

She looked surprised. And flustered, as if she didn't know how to respond. She had to know he was attracted to her, didn't she?

She gazed at him for a moment, then looked away. "Your shirt is soaked. Once I finish mopping up this water we can put it in the dryer."

Yep, still jumpy. "Okay. I'd offer to help but I'm pretty sure once I got down there I wouldn't get back up."

"You've done enough by turning off the water. I tried but it's hard to reach and then I heard the doorbell, so I just left it."

She finished mopping and stood. "I'm going to change. Why don't you put your shirt in the dryer and wait for me in the living room? I won't be long."

He went to the living room and turned on the TV to the History Channel, hoping to find a show that would take his mind off Lana.

She came back wearing jeans and a T-shirt and towel-drying her hair. "Why don't we eat something here instead of going out? My little disaster took up a lot of time. What are you watching?"

"History Channel. I'm a junkie." He flipped off the TV. "You don't have to cook for me."

"Seems like the least I can do since you're going to fix my washer."

He studied her for a moment. Was Lana asking him to stay and have dinner as big a deal as he thought it was? It must mean she trusted him, at least a little. "Okay, you cook, but you have to let me help."

"You're on."

WHAT HAD possessed her to ask Gabe to stay? It would have been a lot less personal to go to a restaurant with him. But once again, she felt guilty because he'd been so nice, not only stopping the flood but offering to fix the stupid washer. So she'd gone with the impulse. And now… She glanced at him, trying not to stare. The only half-naked men Lana had been around in the past year or more had been patients. And that was totally different from having a bare-chested, extremely masculine guy standing in her kitchen.

A man who'd called her beautiful. And the look in his eyes had definitely been appreciative. It would have been the perfect time to flirt a little, and see what happened. But she hadn't done it. Instead she'd pretended like he'd never said a thing.

Still, she wasn't exactly uncomfortable with Gabe. No, she was more… She let her gaze drift over the chest in question. Appreciative. He had a nice chest, with lots of hard, rippling muscles. A really nice chest. And a scar on his side that looked like—

"Lana?" Startled, she jerked her gaze up to his face. "What can I do?"

She stared at him blankly for a minute. *He's talking about cooking, you idiot.* "Is stir-fry all right?"

"Sounds good."

"Why don't you chop some vegetables, then. Here, take a seat at the table and I'll bring them to you." She pulled a couple of peppers, an onion, some broccoli and mushrooms out of the refrigerator and put them on the table along with a cutting board and knife.

She tried to think of a polite way to ask him about his scar, but she couldn't. "When were you shot?"

He looked at her, then at his side. "I'd ask how you knew but I guess when you were a trauma doc you saw a lot of gunshot wounds."

"I worked in an E.R. in Los Angeles. Saturday night knife and gun club." Knives. As always when she thought of knives, she repressed a shudder. Even now, two years later, the image was still vivid. "You don't have to tell me if you don't want to." She took out some chicken, sat beside him and began slicing the meat.

"I don't mind. It happened about six or eight months ago. I got in the way of an abusive husband and his wife." He seeded the pepper, then started cutting it into strips.

"He shot you? Were you involved with her?"

He laughed. "Not me, Cam. The woman was Delilah, Cam's wife."

"Delilah was in an abusive marriage? Good Lord, I had no idea."

"Yeah, he was a real bastard. She tried to divorce him and he didn't much like that idea. Tried to kill her. So she took off and ended up in Aransas City, working for Cam. When the guy caught up to her, I happened to be with her."

"My God, you could have been killed."

"Nah, it was just a flesh wound. Have to admit, though, it hurt like hell."

"I bet. What happened to him?"

"Cam and Maggie came to the rescue and Maggie shot him. I'd passed out by then, but that's what they tell me."

"So you were a hero."

He laughed again. "Not me. That's Cam. Like I said, I just got in the way."

But he'd been the victim of a violent crime. Something they had in common, Lana thought. She finished cutting up the chicken, then took it to the stove and washed her hands. She heard the dryer buzz a minute later and went to get Gabe's shirt. When she came back, Gabe had finished the vegetables and was standing at the sink drying his hands.

She gave him the shirt, then turned on the gas beneath the skillet to begin heating the pan. She felt a pang of disappointment that he was covering up his chest. That was a good sign, she thought. Attraction was a very good sign. Even if she hadn't acted on it, she still felt it.

She tossed in the chicken to stir-fry it before she added the vegetables. "Shouldn't be long."

Gabe was leaning against the countertop, smiling at her. She smiled in return. What was it about him that put her so at ease? That made her feel safe? Because he hadn't rushed her? Hadn't made a move on her? He hadn't even tried to kiss her.

She wondered if he would. And if he did, how would she react?

CHAPTER SEVEN

FRIDAY NIGHT, Gabe took Lana to the Scarlet Parrot. He'd asked her on Monday, while he was fixing her washer. Taking advantage of her gratitude might not have been fair of him, but he figured he would use any leverage he had to ease her into dating.

Delilah spied them as soon as they came in and waved the hostess aside to take care of them herself. "Well, if it isn't my long lost brother-in-law," she said, giving him a hug. "It's about time. We'd just about given up hope you would come in again." She moved away and smiled at Lana. "Hi, Lana."

"Hi, Delilah."

"I told Cam I'd be in," he said. "How's it going, Mom? Where's the belly?"

Damned if her eyes didn't get all teary. "I can't wait until I'm showing. It's wonderful. I don't even mind morning sickness." She hugged him again, so hard she almost knocked him over, then gave him a blinding smile. "Cam's excited, too."

He patted her back and grinned at her. "Yeah, I

caught that when he stopped by the other day. He's really gaga about it all."

"He is, isn't he?" she said, beaming. "I'm sorry," Delilah said to Lana. "We didn't mean to be rude. Cam and I are going to have a baby."

"I gathered that. Congratulations."

"Thanks. We're thrilled. Be sure and talk to Cam before you leave, Gabe." She beamed again and took them to a table, then left to get their drinks.

Lana watched Delilah go with an expression on her face Gabe couldn't quite place. Sad? Or maybe wistful?

"What's wrong?"

She looked at him and smiled, shaking off the sudden mood shift. "Nothing. Why?"

"You looked upset for a minute there. Or sad."

She sighed and rearranged her silverware. "Sometimes I wish you weren't so observant."

So there was a story there. "Meaning you don't want to talk about it." He wished she'd open up to him, but maybe that was too much to expect. She trusted him enough to go out with him. For now, he needed to be content with that.

Delilah came back with their drinks and they both gave their orders. Gabe tried to think of something to say but he didn't think she'd appreciate learning what was on his mind. "You look really beautiful tonight," he said instead. "But then, I think that every time I see you."

Just as she had in her laundry room the other night, she seemed flustered. Finally she stammered, "Th-thank you."

"Why does it make you nervous when I tell you you're beautiful?"

"I'm not nervous." He lifted an eyebrow and she insisted, "I'm not. I'm just not used to men telling me that."

"Why, are they blind?"

She laughed, seeming more at ease. "Thanks. But remember, I haven't been dating. You're the first man I've been out with in…maybe a year."

"What about your ex-husband? He never told you that you're beautiful?" If Gabe was married to her, he'd damn sure let her know he thought she was the prettiest thing he'd ever seen. *Whoa, baby, what the hell was he thinking?* Marriage? Him, married? That was a laugh. He wasn't the marrying type.

She shrugged and sipped her glass of wine. "At first. After we married, he didn't bother much. He was never very…demonstrative." She nodded at the bar. Cam was leaning over it to kiss Delilah. "Like the two of them. He would never have done that." She tightened her lips. "Terence didn't believe in public displays of affection."

"Cam and Delilah are a little sappy," Gabe admitted. "They haven't been married very long, though. Your ex sounds like a stuffed shirt."

She laughed. "He is. Very stuffy."

"So why did you marry him? He doesn't sound like your type."

"I don't know. I thought he was. He was a doctor, so we had medicine in common. We had similar interests, similar goals—or I thought we did. And I loved him. Supposedly he loved me, too." She shrugged and added, "At first, anyway."

Delilah brought their orders, two of the shrimp plates for which the Scarlet Parrot was well-known. She talked with them for a moment, mostly about the baby, then left them to enjoy their meals.

After a little while Lana broke the silence. "She's so happy."

"Delilah? Oh, you mean about being pregnant? Yeah, she and Cam are both goofy about it."

"I don't blame them. Knowing you're having a baby is a feeling like nothing else in the world."

Her tone would have alerted him if her words hadn't. Her expression was sad, infinitely sad. He put down his fork and waited for her to go on.

"But even then, you don't realize just how wonderful it is until it's taken away."

Damn. He reached for her hand, said the only thing he could think of. "I'm sorry, Lana."

"Me, too." She inhaled a shaky breath. "I was four and a half months along when I lost her."

"I'm so sorry," he said again. What else could he say?

She shook her head. "Don't look at me like that. I'm not going to fall apart."

"It wouldn't be a crime if you did. It obviously still hurts."

"Yes. I think it always will. I don't usually talk about it. It makes me sad."

But she'd told him. She'd shared something intensely private with him. "Okay, what do you want to talk about?" He started eating again.

"You. Tell me why you've never been married."

"I don't have anything against it. Exactly. I just never met a woman I wanted to marry."

"No one? You've never been serious about a woman?"

"Serious, no. Gone over, yeah." He put his fork down, rubbed the bridge of his nose, thinking that over. "She was a piece of work. But marriage… It might have crossed my mind, but not seriously. We didn't really last that long, and besides, I was pretty much blinded by the incredible sex."

Lana was looking at him with a funny expression on her face. Damn him and his big mouth. Had he really said that about being blinded by incredible sex?

"Sorry. Sometimes I speak first and think later."

"Don't apologize for being honest."

"A little too honest, sometimes."

"No, I like that about you." She toyed with her food again, then said, "So tell me about this woman you were gone over."

"Maybe later." He smiled cynically. "For now let's just say she was my personal Typhoid Mary."

"You don't sound like you like women much."

"Sure I do. Some women." He picked up her hand and smiled at her. "I like you."

She didn't say anything, she just stared at him. But she didn't pull her hand away.

Delilah came by with the check. At least Cam had kept his word and had told Delilah to let Gabe pay.

"I'm going to the ladies' room," Lana said after Delilah left.

"Okay. I'll be here."

She got up, but before she left she laid her fingers on his arm. "Gabe, just so you know…I like you, too."

He watched her walk away, hips gently swinging. He was getting pretty sappy if something as simple as her saying she liked him made him feel this good.

"DO YOU WANT to go home?" Gabe asked Lana when they left the restaurant.

"Why? Do you have something else in mind?"

"I wondered if you'd like to see my boat. I thought since it's right here, you might."

"I'd love to. I've seen it from a distance, but I've never been in a big boat or even seen one up close."

Though the restaurant parking lot was well-lit, the marina lot was darker, but she slipped her hand into her pocket and managed to remain calm. The feel of the pepper spray canister was reassuring. She was getting better, though. Not as anxious now as she'd been when she first moved. Maybe she was becoming adjusted to the small town. Or maybe it just seemed safer, somehow. When they reached the dock, Gabe turned on a set of lights that illuminated the area.

"It's down this way." He led her to a big white boat with acres of gleaming chrome and shining fiberglass. The name *El Jugador* was painted across the back.

"What does *El Jugador* mean?"

"It's Spanish for 'The Gambler.'"

"So, are you a gambler?"

His mouth lifted at one corner. "Not anymore."

She sensed there was a story behind that but decided she'd ask him later. It took some maneuvering, but they both managed to get into the boat.

"This is the cockpit," Gabe said. "I put chairs out here so people can fish. There's usually a lot of fishing gear around, but Cam brought the stuff to my house since we weren't sure how long I'd be laid up."

He looked sad for a moment, which didn't surprise her. She'd be sad, too, if she faced losing something so important to her. She looked around and sighed. "It's beautiful, Gabe. Lovely."

"It's a boat." He shrugged. "Nothing special. Here, I'll show you the cabin." He unlocked the door and opened it, letting Lana go in first. "This is the main cabin. The couch pulls out to make a double bed. There's a stateroom that sleeps two, so it sleeps four in all. More if you go for sleeping bags on the floor."

It looked like a living room. She could see a narrow kitchen and decided the stateroom must be up under the bow. "Do you often take people out overnight?"

"Sometimes. Especially if there's a tournament. It takes a long time to get to blue water off the Texas coast."

"Did you decorate it yourself?" It was tastefully done in shades of blue and beige. There was a couch, two side chairs and a sturdy wood coffee table.

He laughed. "No, my sisters and my mother got their heads together on that one. I wouldn't have had a clue."

"Is it a full kitchen?"

"We call it a galley on a boat," he said, and motioned her to go in front of him. "It's functional. Stove with an oven. Microwave and refrigerator. Close quarters, though."

There was a hallway that led to a tiny bathroom, or "head," as Gabe called it, and the stateroom. It held a double bed and not much else. She looked at the bed, then looked at Gabe and raised an eyebrow. "Nice bed."

One corner of his mouth lifted. "Legions have thought so."

"Really?"

Their eyes met. "Does it matter?"

He was looking at her, his mouth curving slightly upward, waiting for her answer. Lana panicked. What was she doing, flirting with him this way? When she didn't even know if she could kiss him without showing her fear, much less... She glanced at the bed again then at him. "I'm sorry. It's none of my business."

He held her gaze. "Not legions," he said, ignoring her comment. "Not even close. But there have been a few."

She had no reason to be happy at his response, but she was.

He led the way back into the main cabin. He'd left his cane by the galley door, she assumed because the hallway was so narrow he didn't need it. He stopped and opened the refrigerator. "Want something to drink? A beer or a soft drink?"

"No, I'm fine, thanks."

On his way to the couch he paused to turn on some music, the sound a soft, muted background melody.

"It's a lovely boat, Gabe. No, don't say it's nothing special," she said when he started to speak. "I can see it is." She sat on the couch and he sat beside her, popping the top of his soft drink. He rubbed his leg absentmindedly and she wondered if he'd overdone things showing her around.

"I had an offer from a buyer last Saturday."

So that's what had been wrong with him at the

Kramers' party. No wonder he'd been moody. "And?"

"And it sucked." He drank his soda and frowned.

"Did you take it?"

"No, I turned it down but..." He let the sentence trail off and she finished for him.

"Now you're worried you should have taken it."

He shrugged. "Yeah. Might be the only offer I get."

"Really?"

"No. Well, only when I'm being paranoid. I priced it low as it was."

"Then you did the right thing."

"Maybe. Time will tell."

She wanted to comfort him but she didn't think he'd accept sympathy from her. Instead she asked, "Tell me why you named your boat 'The Gambler.'"

He smiled. "A lot of reasons. It was a gamble to buy it. A gamble to go into the fishing business. But I wanted to try. Turned out to be a good gamble." He drank some more and set the can down. "I almost lost it once before. About seven years ago. No, closer to eight now."

"What happened?"

He turned his head and looked at her. Stared at her, really, as if he were considering just how much he wanted to tell her.

"I used to gamble," he said a long moment later.

"Gamble, as in, you had a problem with gambling?"

He nodded. "I figured you'd have heard by now. It's common knowledge."

"Maggie said—" She hesitated, unsure whether to mention the discussion she'd had with Maggie.

"Maggie told you about it?"

"No. But she said you were snakebit."

Gabe laughed. "That's pretty apt. I just call it bad luck. I wasn't a good gambler. But I had another problem. A five-foot-two, dark-haired kind of problem."

"Ah, a woman."

He smiled cynically. "You got it." He picked up the can, leaned back and drank some more.

"Is this the woman you told me you were gone over?"

"That's her. She was gorgeous. Not just pretty, but drop-dead gorgeous. And young. Sexy little Italian beauty with dark eyes, dark hair and a body that screamed sex. She played me like the biggest, dumbest fish in the ocean. Not that I was much of a challenge. I fell for her. Hard."

Glancing at her, he added, "Usually the beautiful ones go for my brother, not me. Delilah reminded me of her. I gave Delilah a really hard time when she first came here, because of that. But luckily for Cam, Delilah is nothing like Bella."

"Bella?"

"Yeah, Bella." He laughed. "It suited her. Anyway, when Bella let me know she was interested, I jumped right in. Didn't stop to think about what she'd want with me. Hell, I didn't stop to think about anything but how hot she was and how lucky I was that she wanted me, too." He shot her a wry glance. "She wasn't the type to go for a fisherman. Which I'd have known if I'd been thinking with my head instead of my hormones."

He set down the can and sighed. "God, I was stupid."

"No, you weren't stupid. You just trusted the wrong person." As she had when she'd trusted her ex-husband to cope with what had happened to her.

He shrugged. "Anyway, I was so crazy in love, I'd have done anything Bella asked. And I did."

"What did you do?" She put her hand on his knee and patted it in sympathy.

He covered her hand and held it palm-to-palm, resting on his thigh. "You've been in Aransas City long enough to know what it's like. Everyone knows your business. Or thinks they do. So everyone in town knew about my gambling problem." He smiled cynically. "What they don't know is that the gambler was Bella. Oh, I gambled, too, but most of it was her. I wasn't addicted to it, I was just plain dumb. I didn't wise up until I was so deep in debt I was about to lose my boat." He looked at her, waiting for her response.

"Sounds like you picked the wrong woman to fall in love with."

"Yeah. Big-time. Anyway, when I cut off the cash flow, guess what Bella did?"

"Left you."

"Bingo. Took a hike with my cash and credit cards. Ran up several thousand on them before I could stop her. I couldn't even claim fraud, since I'd let her sign on them in the first place. Man, that was a mess."

"Oh, Gabe. I'm sorry."

He rolled a shoulder. "You live and you learn. I managed to turn things around. Took a while, but I've been in the black for a few years now." He hesitated and added, "Or I was."

His thumb was making slow circles on her palm. Soothing but at the same time…arousing. She wondered if he realized it. Glancing at him, she decided he knew exactly what he was doing. She tried to get her mind back to what they were talking about, but it wasn't easy.

"You said everyone thinks you have a gambling problem. I don't understand. Why do you let them believe that when it's not true?"

His grin flashed, bright and quick. "Honey, I did have a gambling problem. Her name was Bella."

"You'd rather people think you have a gambling problem than know—"

He interrupted. "Than know I let a woman make a complete fool out of me? Hell, yes. Anytime."

She stared at him. "Even your family? They don't know the truth?"

"Nope." He shook his head. "Well, I think Cam might suspect, but he doesn't know for sure. We've never talked about it. You're the only person I've ever told."

"Why did you tell me?"

"I wanted you to know the truth, not the rumor."

He was gazing at her so intently, his eyes dark, like liquid chocolate, a faint smile on his mouth.

"Why?" It came out as a whisper.

He brought her hand to his lips while he watched her. Kissed her knuckles, turned it over and kissed her palm. "Because you matter to me, Lana. You're the first woman since then who has."

She couldn't breathe. She didn't know what to say or to do. He was going to kiss her. Really kiss her, and she…she wanted him to.

He smiled at her, let go of her hand and got up. "Come on, I'll take you home."

CHAPTER EIGHT

"DO YOU WANT to come in?" Lana asked Gabe when they pulled up in front of her house.

He turned in the seat and looked at her. She couldn't read his expression. Then he smiled, shook his head, reached out and took her hand. His grasp was solid, warm, reassuring. His hands weren't soft. A lifetime of hard, physical work took care of that. But they were surprisingly gentle. He didn't squeeze her hand, he simply held it. But there was something at work here, and the longer he looked at her with that half-smile, the harder it became for her to breathe.

The night was hot, sultry. He'd rolled down the windows before he turned off the engine. The street was deserted, nearly silent but for the whirr of the cicadas and the occasional soft, deep croak of a frog. The moon flitted in and out of the clouds but there was enough light from that and the porch light she'd left burning to let her see his face.

"Gabe?"

"Yeah, I want to come in. But I'm not going to."

"Why?"

He sighed, let go of her hand and slipped his into her hair. "So soft," he murmured. "I knew it would be. I've been wanting to touch it since the first time I saw you."

"It's just hair." She nearly stuttered. Was he finally, finally, going to kiss her? He ran his fingers through the ends, then put his hand on the back of her neck, buried beneath her hair.

He shook his head and smiled. "More like spun gold. Or silk. There's something else I've wanted to do since the first time I saw you." Gently, so gently, he tugged her forward. His lips closed over hers in a devastatingly slow kiss. She didn't think, didn't analyze, she simply responded. Her lips parted, inviting him in.

There was nothing tentative about his kiss. His lips moved over hers, firm, knowledgeable, setting off little thrills of pleasure as he deepened the kiss and his tongue touched hers. Yet she didn't feel pressured. She knew, beyond a doubt, that if she asked him to stop, he would.

But she didn't want to stop him. She wanted this with an intensity that shocked her. To be an ordinary woman, on an ordinary date. Kissing a man she was very attracted to.

She put her arms around his neck and sank her fingers into the dark hair curling at his nape. Leaned into him and gave a tiny moan when his lips left hers and trailed down her neck, pressing heated kisses into her flesh. He tasted her there, at the rapid pulse at the base of her neck, before taking her mouth again in another deep, drugging kiss.

Her heartbeat sped up, her lips and breasts tingled. His hand slid from her hair down her arm and settled at her waist, urging her closer. She tensed, then forced herself to relax. She didn't think he'd notice, but he did. He lifted his mouth and his hand dropped away, releasing her.

They looked at each other and for the life of her she couldn't think of a thing to say. Gabe didn't speak, either. He got out of the truck and came around to her side, opening her door with manners that seemed ingrained. He remained silent as they went up the walk, as she unlocked the door and stepped inside to turn off the alarm.

"You must wonder—I know it seems—" She stopped, not knowing how to explain what she was feeling, thinking. Was she ever going to be able to put her past behind her? Could she have a normal relationship with a man?

Apparently not. This was the first time Gabe had kissed her and she'd blown it by freezing up. And he'd waited a lot longer than most men would have before even trying.

"You don't owe me an explanation, Lana. Just relax, okay?" He smiled, brushed his knuckles against her cheek. "I'll call you," he said, and left.

But she wondered if he would.

She watched him go, then started her nightly routine. She checked all her doors, checked the alarm, made sure the pepper spray was at her bedside table. Then she changed into her nightgown and got in bed.

She hadn't imagined the importance of what had happened on the boat. Gabe had told her something he'd never told anyone, not even his brother. And he'd said she mattered to him, as no one had since the woman who'd obviously broken his heart.

He mattered to her, too. For the first time since she'd been brutally raped, she had a sense of hope. That someday she might get beyond her past and move on with her life. And that was because of Gabe.

Could Gabe accept what had happened to her and still want her? She had expected her ex-husband to be able to do that, but the man who had supposedly loved her had never been able to get past the rape and the loss of their unborn child.

They hadn't had the perfect marriage before that, but she'd thought they would make it. They were both trying. Maybe she'd been trying harder than Terence but he'd also seemed to want the marriage to work. Then she'd been raped and their marriage hadn't stood a chance. Terence couldn't get past it.

She remembered the first time they tried to make love after the rape. Months after the attack, when she'd finally become tired of his evasions, she'd decided to seduce him. She'd wanted love and intimacy. A memory to replace the violence. Well, she had another memory now, but it wasn't one she'd wanted. And it sure as hell hadn't erased the violence.

Terence couldn't make love to her. He'd tried, when she insisted. And he'd blamed his failure on Lana. He'd said that if she hadn't been so cold, so scared, he wouldn't have failed. She tried to tell herself that Terence's reaction to the rape was his problem, but deep inside she blamed herself as well as him. She hadn't been able to relax, to stop worrying about what would happen if she had a flashback while they made love. Well, she'd never gotten the chance to find out.

But if Terence had been more understanding, more patient, more loving, would that have made a difference? What if he'd been more like Gabe?

Could Gabe help her heal those scars? Or would he turn from her if he knew the truth?

Gabe suspected. He wasn't stupid and she knew she'd given him enough hints.

She should tell him. But right or wrong, she knew she wouldn't. Not yet. She couldn't bear for him to turn from her as Terence had. Gabe suspected what had happened to her, but he didn't *know.* There was a world of difference between suspecting and knowing the grim details. She wouldn't take the chance of losing Gabe, not yet. Maybe not ever.

HE DIDN'T CALL. Not that week and not the next one either. The longer she waited, the more she wondered. Why was he avoiding her? Had he lost interest? Was he mad at her? Had he decided she was too much trouble? Worse, maybe he hadn't been that interested in the first place and she'd just imagined the look in his eyes when he'd said she mattered to him. Imagined him saying he'd wanted to kiss her since he'd first seen her. Imagined that he'd felt something, too, when he did, finally, kiss her.

After a few days of racking her brain about what could have driven him away, she started to get angry. She'd thought they were moving toward something. A relationship of sorts. At the very least, they'd become friends. Friends, with the possibility of being much closer. So why had he suddenly dropped her?

That Friday after work she ran into Cat Kincaid at the dry cleaner's. Cat dropped her clothes off, then waited until Lana had picked hers up and walked out with her.

"I'm glad I ran into you," Cat said. "Mark and I have been meaning to ask you and Gabe to dinner. Are you busy Sunday night?"

It caught her by surprise. "You'd better run that by Gabe first."

"Why? Has he made other plans?"

"I have no idea what Gabe's plans are."

Cat frowned. "I thought you two were dating?"

"Apparently not. We went out a couple of times. No big deal."

Except that it was to her. Gabe was the first person she'd actually dated since those disastrous first few episodes after the divorce, and he'd dropped her without an explanation. Lana opened her car trunk and laid the clothes out before closing it with a little more force than necessary. She wiped a hand across her brow. Five-thirty was the hottest part of the day. Heat radiated up from the asphalt parking lot. No breeze broke the stifling heat.

"So, thanks, Cat, but I'll have to say no."

"Wait, don't go." Cat laid a hand on her arm. "Let's go have a drink and talk."

"I don't—I can't—" She stopped, flustered. She really didn't want to talk to Gabe's sister. After all, she wasn't thinking particularly charitable thoughts about him. She wasn't in the mood to bite her tongue, either.

"Look, just because you and my brother are on the outs, doesn't mean you and I can't be friends. Come on, please? Better yet, we'll have dinner. I'm starved. Or do you have other plans?"

"No. Just Friday night in front of the TV."

"We can bash him together. I swear, I won't say one good thing about him."

Lana smiled reluctantly. "You don't have to go that far. All right. Where?"

"Since I gather you don't want to run into Gabe,

I guess the Parrot's out. How about we try the Mexican place on Main Street?"

"I'll meet you there. But—" She hesitated, torn between wanting to talk to another woman and feeling as if she was imposing. "What about your family? Aren't they expecting you for dinner?"

"Nope," she said cheerfully. "The kids are with my mother for the weekend. And Mark is working late, so I'm free as a bird. Tonight, anyway." She smiled wickedly and added, "Tomorrow I'm going to enjoy a child-free day and night with my husband. Which is why I'd asked you and Gabe to come Sunday night."

A short time later they were seated in the restaurant with chips and hot sauce in front of them. Cat ordered a margarita and cheese enchiladas, and Lana ordered a Mexican beer and fajitas.

"So," Cat said after the waiter brought their drinks. "What's going on with you and Gabe?"

"Nothing." She took a sip of beer and continued. "We went out a few times and then he stopped calling." As soon as he'd kissed her and she had frozen, she added silently.

"For no reason?" Cat persisted. "He just stopped calling, out of the blue?"

"More or less." She was unwilling to go into details, especially with his sister.

"You didn't have a fight."

Lana shook her head.

"That's weird." Looking perplexed, she picked up her drink and sipped it. "I can only drink half or I won't be able to drive home. I'm a real light-weight." She set the glass down and picked up a chip. "I used to tease Gabe that the women he dated had IQs the same as their bra sizes."

Lana choked on her drink, then laughed. "Ah, I don't think that describes me."

"No." She dipped a chip in hot sauce, then ate it. "Which was why Gail and I were so pleased when you two started going out. And I can tell you one thing, Cam says Gabe's crazy about you."

"Cam is obviously behind the times."

"Do you care?"

"Cat, I—"

"I know, I know," she interrupted. "I'm his sister, so you feel really uncomfortable bashing him. But it's okay. If you care about him and he's being an idiot I want to know why. He seemed happier when you two started going out than he's been since the accident."

Lana sighed. She wanted to talk to someone and Cat seemed prepared to listen. "I don't understand him. We—I thought we were getting along fine."

"Why don't you ask him?"

"Ask him?"

"Yeah, ask him what's wrong. He'll tell you. Gabe has a big mouth. He's constitutionally incapable of keeping anything to himself."

Unless it was important, she thought, remembering the story about Bella. The story he'd told no one but her. "You think I should just go over to his house and ask him."

"Sure." Cat picked up her fork and enthusiastically dug into the food the waiter had just set in front of them. "Or you could be subtle. Take him some cookies or something. Believe me, if you feed Gabe cookies he'll tell you anything you want to know."

"Cookies, huh?" Lana smiled. "What kind of cookies?"

CHAPTER NINE

GABE KNEW he was being a jerk. He should have called Lana. But when he'd kissed her the other night, finally held her in his arms and kissed her like he'd wanted to since the first time he'd seen her, everything had crystallized. It didn't matter how long he'd known her. Didn't matter that he'd never even kissed her until the other night. No, dammit, none of that mattered. He was centimeters away from falling in love with her.

Which scared the hell out of him. He didn't want to fall in love with Lana. Didn't want to be in love with any woman. Not now, when his life was such a train wreck. When he didn't have a job and didn't have a clue what he was going to do for the rest of his life.

Besides, he didn't trust love. The one time he'd really fallen in love with someone, she'd done a tap dance on his heart in stiletto heels. Not that he thought Lana was at all like Bella. She wasn't a shallow gold digger. No, she was far more dangerous than Bella had ever been. Because she wasn't a woman he could take lightly.

He should have known he was in trouble the minute he'd started blabbing to her about Bella. He'd lost his mind, that was his problem.

So when he'd gotten home, he'd thought long and hard and decided the only way to handle the problem was to not see Lana anymore. He convinced himself that was what she wanted. She wasn't sure about him anyway. She'd frozen when he kissed her, for crying out loud. She obviously didn't want to get involved with him, she'd had to be conned into dating him in the first place. So he didn't call.

But man, was it hard. And he was frustrated. So he lifted weights. A lot. His physical therapist was surprised, not to mention happy, about the progress. Gabe could have told him that exercise was the only thing keeping him from losing his mind.

When his doorbell rang Saturday morning he thought about ignoring it, but since it was bound to be one of his family, he knew the uninvited caller would continue to ring the bell until Gabe answered. He finished the set and placed the bar back on the rack.

He mopped his face and chest with a towel before slinging it around his neck, then grabbed his cane and limped to the front door. He opened it and stood there in shock. Lana. The very woman he'd been trying to forget.

"Hi," Lana said. "Have I come at a bad time?"

Yes, he thought. "No," he said. She wore a pale

yellow T-shirt, short white shorts and sandals. She looked absolutely good enough to eat. He groaned mentally and stood aside to let her in. His gut said to grab her and kiss that sexy mouth. His mind said to back off. But damn, he wanted her. Obviously he hadn't done enough reps with the weights.

"I've interrupted you," she said, but she walked in and handed him a brown paper bag. "I hope it's all right. I made cookies."

He looked inside the bag and smiled. "Sugar cookies. My favorite." He took one out and bit into it. It was melt-in-your-mouth good, which didn't surprise him. Lana was the type to do everything well.

"I know. Cat told me."

He had to wait until he'd finished the cookie before he spoke. She'd baked cookies, especially for him. If she kept doing things like that, he'd lose his resolve to keep his distance. "These are good. You asked my sister what kind of cookies I like?"

"Yes. Why, is that a problem?"

"Not if you don't mind the news being all over town that you and I are an item."

She laughed. "Because I baked you cookies?"

"Because Cat knows you baked me cookies. Which means she'll tell Gail and before you know it, the whole town will know. Add that to the fact that you've gone out with me a couple of times and the grapevine will be buzzing at top speed."

"Would it be so bad for people to think that you and I are…together?"

"Not if it were true. But it's not, is it? We're not really dating, I'm just your buffer against blind dates and pushy men."

"So that's why you haven't called. Is that what you really think? Is that honestly how you think I see you?"

"If it looks like a duck and quacks like a duck, it usually is a duck."

Lana looked at him speculatively then said, "Were you working out?"

Change of subject. Fine with him. "Lifting weights."

"Need some help? I can spot you."

He shrugged again and limped out of the room into the spare bedroom that held the weight bench, barbells and dumbbells, and not much else. Anything was better than looking at her, wanting her and knowing he couldn't have her. Abusing his body with exercise might give him some peace of mind.

He tossed his cane aside and lay down on the bench before picking up the long, weighted bar to do a series of chest presses. Lana stood behind him, smiling as she watched him, waiting to see if he needed her help. Her presence shot his concentration all to hell. He finished the first set without help and added more weight. He lay down again and began another.

"I had an ulterior motive for coming over," she said after a minute.

Ten, eleven, twelve. Lana spotted him the last two reps as he heaved the bar onto the rack. "What ulterior motive?" he asked.

Her T-shirt gaped when she leaned over. He could see her white, lacy bra, the swells of her breasts above it. He groaned and closed his eyes.

"I wanted to ask you something."

"Ask away."

"Are you mad at me?"

"No. Why would I be?" Opening his eyes, he thanked God for the fact that she'd straightened and removed temptation from his line of vision. He picked up the bar and started another series.

"Because of what you said earlier. That I think of you as a buffer. I haven't seen you for two weeks, or heard from you, so I wondered."

Mad at her? He wanted to take her to bed, to strip off her clothes and make love to her. Wanted to hear her call his name as she came. Wanted to—

Forget it, he told himself. He picked up the bar and lifted it, brought it close to his chest and pushed it back out.

As he neared the end of the reps, she leaned forward again. Her shirt gaped exactly as it had done before, and he struggled to replace the bar, his eyes drawn inexorably to her breasts. He could see the dark shadow of her nipples through the bra. God, he wanted to touch her so much, cup those sweet breasts, taste her…

A better man would know she didn't realize what she was showing him. A better man would tell her not to lean over. God knew, he wasn't that man. No, he intended to look his fill, torture as it was to look and know he couldn't touch.

"Are you sure you're okay?" she asked, helping him guide the bar to the rack. "You look sort of funny."

Funny wasn't the word he'd use. Aroused. Frustrated. Tense. Aching. Any of those words would do. "I'm fine. And I'm not mad at you." He sat up and wiped off his chest and arms, resting a moment before picking up twenty-five-pound dumbells to begin biceps curls.

Lana came around and sat beside him on the bench. Her perfume drifted to him, a light floral scent that smelled like spring rain. "When I was in California, I did some weight training. I'd forgotten how much I enjoyed it. Watching you work out reminds me of that."

"Why'd you quit?" He curled his forearm up and back down, glad that he had something in his hands to stop him from grabbing what he really wanted to hold.

"No gym in Aransas City. I guess I could look around to see if there's one over in Port Aransas. Or I could buy a bench and some weights." She watched him and when he started on the other arm said, "Have you been training long?"

"Just since the accident. Before that, I never did." After a fishing trip he was generally too tired to do much except fall into bed and sleep.

"Your job kept you in shape."

He grimaced as he curled his arm. "Fishing's more physical than most people think."

"You have to be pretty tough to wrestle a two- or three-hundred-pound fish, I suppose. Marlins get that big and bigger, don't they?"

He shot her a sideways glance and grinned. "You've been reading up."

She smiled back. "It's amazing what you can find out on the Internet."

He felt ridiculously pleased that she'd been researching fishing. Maybe she really did care, at least a little. He set the dumbells down and wiped the towel over his forehead, ready for a break. "I used to be a bouncer at a dive in Port Aransas. The jokers I had to get rid of always weighed twice what I did. And when they were drunk, they got mean, and they were always drunk. Compared to that, fishing's easy."

"You were a bouncer?"

"Yeah." He rolled a shoulder. "The pay was decent and I needed the money to save for a down payment on my boat. And that wasn't by any stretch the worst job I ever took." She was looking at him as if he were a different species. Well, compared to the men she was used to, he was. He bet her ex-husband had never dirtied his hands with tossing out drunks from a bar or working on a shrimper.

"What's wrong, Doc?" he asked mockingly. "You have a problem dating a man who used to knock people's heads together for a living?"

"Don't do that. Don't try to put distance between us by making me out a snob."

"I don't think you're a snob. But admit it. I'm blue-collar." He traced a finger down her cheek. "And you, baby, are white-collar all the way." He had to consciously move his hand away before he sank it into her hair, dragged her close and kissed her until she couldn't breathe.

"Is that why you quit calling me?"

Better if she thought that was his reason, but he didn't like lying to her. "No."

"Why didn't you call me, Gabe?"

"You don't want to go there, Lana."

"Yes. I do. Even if it's because you were bored with me and our…friendship, I want to know. I need to know. Please."

Oh, hell, what was he supposed to do now? Tell her he'd fallen in love with her? Yeah, that would send her running so fast he'd be eating her dust. So he settled on another reason, though not the main one.

"I don't think you really want to see me. So I made it easy on you. I didn't call."

She looked at him blankly. “I don’t understand. We’ve been dating.”

“I’ve been dating,” he pointed out. “You had to be conned into it.”

“That’s not true, Gabe. I wouldn’t have gone if I hadn’t wanted to.”

“I think you would have. I think you were trying to prove it wasn’t a mercy date when it was.”

Her mouth fell open, then she snapped it closed. “Don’t be ridiculous. I’ve never known anyone less in need of a mercy date than you.”

He grinned at her irritable tone. “Thanks. I have to tell you, my ego thanks you, too.”

“I kissed you. If it had been a mercy date, I wouldn’t have.”

“Technically, I kissed you.”

She pressed her lips together. “Are you trying to annoy me? Because you’re doing a good job of it.”

He laughed. “Trust me, darlin’, annoying you is the last thing I want to do.” No, he wanted to eat her up in great big bites. Starting from the top and working his way down.

“Then trust *me*. If I hadn’t wanted you to kiss me, you’d never have gotten near me.”

He suspected that was true. He realized she wasn’t talking anymore but was staring at him with a look in her eyes that in another woman he might have thought was lust. Yeah, right. Wishful thinking.

She touched her tongue to her lips. “There’s

something I've wanted to do since I got here." Raising her hands, she placed her palms flat on his chest. "Do you mind?"

Mind? Did he mind that she looked as though she was about to make his fantasies come true? "That's a rhetorical question, right?"

She laughed, a sexy little gurgle, and, spreading her fingers, ran her hands slowly over his chest. Her fingers grazing his nipples, her palms smoothing over his muscles. This was too good—it had to be a dream.

"I thought you'd feel like this," she murmured. "I wanted to put my hands on you this way since I walked in and saw you without your shirt. You've got great…muscular definition. Strong. Hard."

Hard? He was beyond hard. And he'd been that way since before she'd ever touched him. She leaned forward and kissed him, slipping her tongue into his mouth to tease, taunt. No hesitation, no uncertainty.

He put his arms around her and pulled her against him, sliding his tongue against hers in a slow, seductive rhythm. She didn't freeze, didn't pull back. Instead she snuggled against him, moving her hands down to his waist so her soft, amazing breasts were pillowed against his bare chest.

He slipped one hand into her hair, angling her head so he could kiss her more deeply. Some part of him waited for her to stop him, for her to get cold feet, but she didn't. Her arms slid up his back, slowly caressing him as she continued to exchange soul-searing kisses with him. Finally he had to stop or risk taking her right there on the weight bench. And he wanted her in his bed. He just wasn't at all sure she was ready to be there.

"Lana."

"Hmm?" She smiled at him and ran her tongue over her lips. Started to pull his head back down to hers.

His mind blanked for a moment. "I want to make love to you."

She said nothing, but she stared at him so long he knew he'd blown it. "Forget I said that. It's too soon. I shouldn't have—"

"Gabe." She put her fingers to his lips and smiled. "Yes."

"Yes?"

"Yes. I want you to make love to me."

Did she really? If she was going to back out, he'd rather she did so now than later. "I need to take a shower." He rubbed a hand over his jaw that hadn't seen a razor in days. "And shave."

She looked a little dazed. "Why?"

He kissed her, but lightly this time. "I don't want to give you razor burn."

"Don't...go. I don't care about that."

"What's wrong, Lana? Afraid you'll change your mind if you have time to think about it?"

She was silent for a moment. "What if I did? What

if I was gone when you came out?" Her eyes were locked on his earnestly.

"Then I'd have to turn around and get back into the shower—a very cold shower." He kissed her again, quick and just a little hard. "I want you to be sure. I'm not going to make love to you unless you're as sure as I am that you want to be there. In my bed."

"Most men wouldn't take that chance."

Most men weren't in love with her, which he sure as hell didn't plan to tell her. "I told you once that you matter to me. I meant it."

He started to get up and his leg buckled, forcing him to fall back on the bench.

His damned leg. He'd forgotten all about it. He closed his eyes and sucked in a breath, willing the pain away.

Opening his eyes, he gave Lana a bitter smile. "Now wasn't that just romantic as hell?"

She put her hand on his bad leg and touched it gently, her eyes solemn on his. "Gabe, it doesn't matter."

"It matters to me." He wanted to be normal again. Strong and…whole, dammit. Instead of damn near helpless. Once, he'd have thought nothing of picking her up and carrying her into his bedroom. Now he couldn't even get himself there without help.

Lana kept stroking his leg, running her fingers over the road map of scars. Not saying anything, just looking at him.

He grabbed her hand and stilled it. "Don't," he said harshly. She was so…perfect. And he was anything but.

"They're just scars, Gabe," she said softly. "I have them, too. Mine just aren't as visible."

How could he have forgotten? This wasn't all about him. It was about Lana. He was dead certain by now that she'd been raped, and almost as sure that she hadn't made love since. He wanted to remind her what sex could be like, and make her forget the nightmare that had happened to her. And he wanted to make love to her because he wanted her so much it was nearly killing him.

"Maybe you should carry me."

Her smile broke like sunrise over the ocean. "I would, but I don't think that's going to work. But you can lean on me, can't you?"

"Leaning on you wasn't exactly what I had in mind."

She got up and held out her hands. He put his into them and let her help him up. Once he was standing, she slipped her arms around his waist and raised her face for his kiss. He bent his head and took her mouth, spread his hands over her bottom and pulled her tight against him.

"I guess you're still interested," she murmured against his mouth.

"Baby, you have no idea." They made their way slowly down the hall, stopping every few minutes to kiss and caress each other.

Eventually they reached his bedroom and tumbled onto the bed. He landed between her legs, his arousal pressed against the softest, warmest part of her. And she froze.

He wanted so much to stay where he was, nestled against her so intimately. But she needed time to think things through, and he meant to give it to her. He rolled off her and looked down at her, smiling. "Are you going to be here when I get back?"

"I think so. I hope so." She raised her hand, cupped his cheek. "Gabe—"

He turned his head and kissed her palm. "What?" he asked huskily.

"I don't want to…disappoint you."

Was she kidding? He stared at her, trying to read her expression. She was serious. Dead serious. How could a woman like Lana doubt herself so much? He kissed her lips. "Lana, there is no possible way you're going to disappoint me." He took her hand and pressed it to his arousal. "Does that feel like disappointment?"

She stroked him, her smile growing as his erection did. "No, it doesn't."

"There's just one thing," he said, concentrating on not exploding beneath her caressing hand. "When we make love—" He slipped his hand behind her hair to her nape, pulled her mouth to his and kissed her. "You have to be on top."

Without giving her a chance to speak, he got up

and limped into the bathroom. "You're a dumb-ass," he told himself, looking in the mirror. "You should have taken her when you had the chance." If he was still a gambling man, he'd have bet the entire farm she'd be gone when he came out.

CHAPTER TEN

FOR A FEW MINUTES after Gabe went into the bathroom, Lana simply lay on his bed, unable to believe he'd actually left her. She didn't know of a single other man who would have, especially knowing she might be gone when he came out.

But Gabe had been surprising her ever since she'd met him. He must want more than a simple fling with her if he was willing to go to so much trouble to make certain of her feelings.

She sat up and looked around the room, curious to learn more about him. The bedroom was unabashedly masculine. A few pieces of dark furniture with clean lines filled the medium-size room. The bed was unmade and very comfortable. Only one picture graced the walls, a framed picture of his boat, taken out on the water at sunset, the red sun a fitting background for the gleaming white vessel.

The room was neat, no clothes tossed in the corners and very little stuff lying around. She'd imagined that a long-time bachelor would be messier.

A number of books, several of them hardbacks, lay on the bedside table, a couple of them open and the rest stacked neatly. Curious to see what he read in his spare time, she picked one up. A book on Texas history. Glancing at the others, she realized all of them were some sort of history book, from American history to Asian and European. She remembered that he had admitted to being a history junkie. She'd never have guessed that a man who professed to hate school would have such an obvious love of history.

She thought she heard a sound but the door remained firmly closed. He'd hardly had time to shower, much less shave. Troubled, she set the book down. Soon, he'd come through that door. And he would expect to make love to her. Expect her to be ready, to be sure of what she was doing, when she was anything but.

Could she go through with it? Risk getting hurt, and worse, risk hurting him? If she left…no matter what he'd said, she knew their budding relationship would be over. No man would put up with a woman who couldn't make up her mind. A woman who blew hot one minute and cold the next.

But if she stayed, what if she failed? Failed, as she had in the past. What if she had a flashback or froze or did something else to turn him off? What if she couldn't respond to him as he wanted her to?

She'd responded earlier, but she hadn't had time to think about it, to worry. Oh, why hadn't he just made love to her when she'd asked him to?

Terence had told her often enough that she was the one at fault. That her problems had ruined the relationship, not his. She could still hear his words, each time they'd tried and Terence couldn't make love to her. *Face it, Lana, you're the problem. My God, you flinch every time I touch you. How is any man supposed to make love to a woman who can't respond? To a woman who's as frigid as an ice cube.*

She knew she was partially to blame. She could admit that now. It was unrealistic to expect that something as traumatic as rape wouldn't have an effect on her sex life. But she'd wanted to work through her problems, and Terence had been irritated by them. So Terence had been at fault, too. He hadn't seemed to be able to understand why she couldn't just "get past it." At first he'd been sympathetic. But the longer it went on, the more impatient he'd become with her. The more angry he grew for what he saw as her rejection of him. Then he'd left her for his counselor and after that, she hadn't trusted any man. Didn't believe any man would want her enough to be patient.

But Gabe did want her. And he was clearly aware she had some issues, even if he didn't know exactly what they were.

You didn't freeze in the other room, she reminded herself. *And you want Gabe, you know you do.* She'd been fine…for a little while. Until they'd come into the bedroom and she'd felt him on top of her.

She closed her eyes. God, she was hopeless. Gabe deserved better than a woman who might never be able to have a normal relationship with a man. She gave the closed door one last look, then got up and left.

Lana was gone when he came out of the bathroom. Gabe wasn't surprised. He'd been almost sure she would take off. But had she left because of him, because of something he'd said or done? Or had she left because she was scared, because she hadn't been ready?

Whatever the reason, he was going after her. He'd tried to forget her and it hadn't worked. He might as well face the fact that he was falling in love with her and wanted a chance with her, even though he knew the odds were astronomical that they'd ever last. At least he could try. And he had to let her know, since she obviously didn't, that she didn't have to run away from him. All she needed to do was to tell him she wasn't ready.

Half an hour later, he rang her doorbell. He heard the beat of heavy metal even through the closed door, so he rang it again. It made him smile. He hadn't figured Lana for a heavy-metal-type woman. Classical, jazz, something like that, but never heavy metal. The music died down and she opened the door, looking totally shocked.

"Can I come in?" he asked when she simply stood there staring at him.

She stepped back and let him in, closing the door behind him. "I didn't expect to see you."

"I figured that. That's why I came over."

"I'm sorry I—" She closed her eyes and bit her lip. "I'm sorry I ran out on you."

"We need to talk."

She motioned to the couch and he limped over to it. It took him a minute to get there. God, it was annoying to never be able to do things easily. Even something as simple as sitting on a couch. He blew out a breath and propped his leg in front of him before he looked at her. "Why did you leave?"

She clasped her hands together on her lap and looked down. She wouldn't meet his eyes. "I realized…I'm not ready to…make love. I know my actions made it seem like…I was. But I'm just not," she finished hesitantly.

"Lana." He waited until she looked up. "It's okay to tell me that. I'm not going to push you into doing something you're not sure about. That's why I gave you a chance to think about it. But you didn't have to take off. All you had to do was tell me you'd changed your mind."

"I couldn't. I was embarrassed. I didn't think you'd want me there. Not after I'd—" She stopped and her jaw hardened. "Damn it, I came on to you. And then I ran out. At the least, I thought you'd be angry."

"Do I look angry?"

She considered him. “No, you don’t.”

“Because I’m not. I told you I was giving you a chance to think it over.”

“I guess I didn’t believe you really meant it.” She looked down at her hands, then back at him. “But you did, didn’t you?”

“Yeah, I meant it. I’d never hurt you, Lana. Not on purpose.”

“I…know.”

“Do you?” She nodded, but hesitantly. He wasn’t at all sure she believed that. But he meant to convince her. “Do something for me.”

“What?”

“Talk to me. Next time you’re feeling rushed, just tell me. You don’t have to run off.”

She was silent for a moment, just looking at him. “What if I’m never ready?”

He smiled and traced his thumb over her mouth. “We’re not on a timetable here, Lana. We’ll just take it slow and see what happens.”

He put his arms around her and pulled her close. Smoothed a hand up her back and over her soft, silky hair. Inhaled her scent of flowers after a spring rain. She rested her head against his shoulder, relaxed into him in a way that brought a lump to his throat. God, she was making him sappy. He felt like he was swimming in deep water, with no life preserver.

“I’m a jerk,” he murmured. “I shouldn’t have quit calling you.”

"It's okay." She slipped her arms around his waist. "When you quit calling, I thought you'd lost interest."

He chuckled again. "No chance of that. Why do you think I've been lifting weights?"

"Physical therapy?"

"Nope. I was trying to get you out of my mind. It didn't work."

"I'm glad," she said.

"Me, too." He pulled back and looked at her. "Let's try this again. We'll take it as slow as you want. You call the shots. Okay?"

She looked troubled. "That doesn't seem fair to you."

"Let me worry about that." He kissed her, careful to make it light, easy, nonthreatening. "So, is it a deal?"

She smiled and put her hand on his cheek. "You scare me."

"That wasn't exactly what I wanted to hear."

"You scare me because you tempt me. I haven't been tempted in a long time. So long I'd almost forgotten what it was like. To want…someone."

"Good." He kissed her again, a little longer, a little slower. Then he forced himself to end the kiss and hold her.

"Gabe?" She pulled back and gazed up into his face. "Why are you being so patient with me? Most men would have blown me off a long time ago."

He looked into those deep-sea eyes and went down for the third time. Don't tell her, he thought. She's not ready for that, either. Hell, neither was he. But when he opened his mouth the truth came out.

"I'm in love with you, Lana."

HER PHONE RANG. She didn't make a move to answer it, she only stared at Gabe in shock. "What did you say?"

He half smiled. "Just what you thought I said. You'd better answer that."

"The answering machine will get it. Gabe—"

He picked up her hands, held them together and kissed them. "Answer the phone. We'll talk later."

She hesitated but then she heard her ex-sister-in-law's voice on the machine. They still kept in touch because, as Crystal put it, "Just because my brother is an idiot doesn't mean I am. You'll always be family to me. Besides, you're Dani's godmother and nothing will change that."

"Hi, Cris," she said, interrupting the message she was leaving. "Sorry, I couldn't get to the phone in time. What's up?"

She shot a glance at Gabe but he hadn't moved. He was watching her, smiling as if he hadn't just dropped the biggest bomb she could think of on her. Gabe loved her? Damn, now she'd totally lost track of what Cris was saying.

"What? I didn't hear that."

Cris laughed. "That's no wonder with Dani screeching in my ear. Dani wanted to thank you for her birthday present."

Before she could answer, her goddaughter demanded the phone. "I miss you, Aunt Lana. When are you coming to see me?"

Her heart melted at the sound of the little girl's voice. She'd been there when Dani was born seven years before and had seen a lot of her over the years. In fact, Dani and Cris were about the only people in California that she missed. "I don't know, punkin. I have to work, so I can't tell when I'll be able to come. I miss you, too."

"I have a new cousin," the little girl announced. "But Aunt Janelle says I'm not old enough to hold him. I don't think that's fair, do you?"

Lana felt as if she'd turned to ice. Dani kept chattering but Lana didn't hear any of the words. A baby. Her ex-husband now had a child. A baby she hadn't been able to give him. She'd wanted to try again when she'd recovered from the miscarriage, but Terence had killed that hope—each and every time he'd rejected her. And with every rejection, her heart had withered a little more. Her stomach churned. She wanted to throw up.

"Lana?" Cris said, coming back on the line. "Oh, God, sweetie, I'm sorry. It didn't occur to me Dani would blurt out that news."

"I-it's…all right. I was just surprised," she lied,

thankful she'd managed to speak. It wasn't all right. She wanted to die.

"I would have told you before you came out here but I didn't see any reason to say anything until I had to. I'm such an idiot, I should have warned Dani. I'm so sorry," she said again. "I wouldn't have had you find out this way for anything."

"Don't worry about it. Listen, Cris, I have to go. I'll call you." Blindly, she hung up.

"Lana, what's wrong?" Gabe asked. He'd gotten up and come to her, and now he grasped her arm, looking at her with concern. "What's wrong, honey?" he repeated.

"Nothing." Her stomach was turning somersaults. She couldn't think about it now. If she did, she'd fall apart. She hated that Terence still had the power to hurt her. After what she'd been through, why would this one thing hurt so much?

Because Terence had a child now. And because she still desperately mourned the one she'd lost.

"You look like you've been poleaxed. Tell me what's wrong. Is someone hurt?"

I am, she thought. But she couldn't speak. She simply shook her head. She stared into his eyes, seeing such sweet concern, such tenderness, she nearly cried. But she was afraid if she started, she'd never stop. She didn't want to think about her ex-husband and the fact that while he so clearly had gone on with his life, she hadn't.

Gabe could help her. Help her heal, help her start her life anew. If she let him. All she had to do was refuse to let fear and insecurity rule her. She put her arms around his neck, pulled his head down to hers and kissed him. He returned the kiss but then pulled back and looked at her, clearly puzzled.

"Make love to me, Gabe."

CHAPTER ELEVEN

GABE STARED AT HER. "You want me to…you want—" Unable to finish the sentence, he broke off.

"I want to make love with you, Gabe. Now."

She not only sounded desperate, she looked shell-shocked. He shook her off and backed away awkwardly. "Not ten minutes ago you said you weren't ready. In fact, forty-five minutes ago, you were so *not* ready, you pulled a disappearing act."

"I changed my mind."

His eyes narrowed and he frowned. "What was that phone call about?"

Her laugh was devoid of humor. "Let's just say it was a wake-up call."

"Lana—"

"Do you want to make love or not?" She reached for the hem of her T-shirt and before he could blink, yanked it off over her head. When her hands went to her shorts, he managed to move, reaching her in a few halting, stumbling steps.

Thank God he reached her before she could get

those off, too. He'd dreamed about undressing her, but not like this. He wanted her warm and willing, not upset and frantic.

He put his hands over hers and stilled them, keeping his eyes firmly on her face. No way was he going to look any lower. He was nowhere near that strong.

"What the hell is going on with you, Lana? Don't tell me you've suddenly been overcome by lust, because I won't believe it."

Silently she gazed at him. Tears welled in her eyes and tracked slowly down her cheeks. Damn. He didn't know what to do. Feeling helpless, he pulled her into his arms and placed her head against his chest, patting her back, murmuring soothing nothings to her as she cried.

He tried desperately not to think about the fact that he held a half-naked, gorgeous—and sobbing—woman in his arms. The very woman he'd dreamed about day and night for weeks. But that was impossible. Every inch of him knew he was holding Lana, and every inch of him wanted her with an intensity he hadn't felt in years. Maybe ever.

Eventually she stopped crying. He slid his hands up her arms and looked down at her. She didn't, as he'd expected, look beautiful when she cried. Her nose was red, her peaches-and-cream complexion splotchy, her eyes swollen. He wanted to make the hurt go away, wanted to protect her from whatever had caused her such pain. She still hadn't spoken, but was looking at him with such sorrow, his heart twisted.

"Do you want to talk about it?"

Gazing into his eyes, she shook her head. "I don't want to talk. Kiss me, Gabe."

He lowered his head and took her mouth slowly, gently. She sighed and leaned into him. She tasted of tears, but something more. Something sweet, a little hesitant. She smelled so good, like a field of flowers, and she felt even better with her barely covered breasts snuggled up against his chest. Her mouth opened and her tongue sought his, moving in a slow, sexy rhythm that skyrocketed the kiss from hesitant to hot.

Somehow, they made it to the couch, though how he managed it without falling over, he didn't really know. He sank down and settled Lana on his lap, kissing her while she wrapped her arms around his neck and pressed herself into him. If they didn't stop soon, there would be no stopping at all.

He broke the kiss and stared at her. Her lips were full, moist from his kisses, her eyes heavy-lidded. She was beautiful again, unbelievably desirable. His for the taking. Hard to believe that less than an hour before she'd run out of his place because she wasn't ready to make love.

Gabe wanted to make love to her more than he'd ever wanted anything. But not like this. Not while she was so upset she was reeling and desperately looking for a way to forget whatever had devastated her.

He'd never made love to a woman he cared about as much as he did Lana. He wanted their first time to be special, to mean something to her, as it would him. He wanted her to want him, not just need the oblivion sex could bring.

"Talk to me, Lana. Tell me what's wrong."

"I don't want to talk." She looked into his eyes and then her gaze fell. "You don't want me, do you?"

Not want her? He could have pulled out his hair. "You have to know I do. But our first time should be about you and me, not about whatever's got you so upset."

She stared at him, then closed her eyes and shook her head. "I'm sorry." She leaned her head against his shoulder and sighed. "I'm doing it again. Using you to help me deal with…things. I can't believe I did that. You must think I'm awful."

"I don't think you're awful." He rubbed his hand up her arm. "You're upset and you turned to me for comfort. But we don't have to have sex for you to feel better. So tell me what happened. What was that call about?"

HE WAS RIGHT. She would have regretted it if they'd made love simply because she was upset about her ex-husband. And Gabe deserved better than that, too. Lana got up and walked over to pick up her shirt. She pulled it over head. "I don't want to think about it."

"Uh-huh." He looked at her a minute. "Is that working?"

"It was," she said. Then blew out a breath. "Okay, not really," she admitted. She went back to the couch and sat beside him.

He didn't say anything else. Just waited patiently for her to make the next move.

"I found out my ex-husband just had a baby. With his new wife."

"Damn. That must have been hard to hear."

Throat tight, she nodded. "It shouldn't have been such a shock. I knew—" She'd known Terence wanted children. The child she'd lost had only widened the wedge between them. "I knew he wanted children. They're both in their thirties. I should have realized…"

"Are you still in love with him?"

"No." He didn't speak, but she felt his skepticism. "It's not him. It's…I told you I lost a child. I know this probably makes me a horrible person, but—" She broke off, not wanting to voice her thoughts.

"Being upset because you lost your baby doesn't make you horrible, Lana."

"No, but what I'm thinking does." Tears stung her eyes. "It hurts." She clenched a fist, wanting to pound something. "Dammit, it's not fair. He has a new wife, a new baby, and I'm left with nothing. Except memories." She closed her eyes wishing she could stop the bombardment of emotion.

Gabe pulled her closer, kissed her hair. "You're right. It's not fair."

She leaned into him, accepting the comfort he offered. "I was so happy when I found out I was pregnant. And carrying the baby—" She laughed. "I know it's cliché, but I really never felt better. We were both happy. Even though we'd been having problems, we both wanted the baby. I thought having a child would bring us closer. And she did. Or at least, I believed that she did."

But now, after all this time, Lana wasn't so sure. Had she and Terence really grown closer, or was that just a fantasy she'd conjured to torment herself further? Everything would have been all right if only she hadn't lost the baby…if only she'd never been raped. But maybe none of those things had caused them to separate. Maybe she and Terence had simply not been right for each other.

Gabe said nothing, just kissed her hair again and tightened his arm around her. Rubbed a hand up her arm comfortingly.

"I really believed we were going to make it. And then I—" Her throat closed up but she forced herself to continue. "I got an infection and had a miscarriage." She could still feel the horror and despair, when, just weeks after the rape she went into labor and lost the baby. Her doctor had said the premature labor was caused by the infection. An infection most likely caused by the rape.

"Wait a minute." Looking at her, he frowned. "You're not blaming yourself for the miscarriage, are you?"

She didn't answer. Because she did. If only she'd gotten security to walk with her that night...

He pushed her chin up so she would look at him. "I don't know much about pregnancies, but my sister Gail had a miscarriage scare. She didn't lose the baby but she was afraid she would and was blaming herself because she had fallen. The doctor said it wasn't her fault, that she couldn't have caused it."

"It's not the same. I can't explain it." Because as close as they'd become, she still couldn't tell him about the rape. She didn't know if she'd ever be able to.

"You're a doctor. You should know better than to blame yourself for something you couldn't help. Women have miscarriages all the time for all sorts of reasons. It wasn't your fault, Lana."

His voice was deep and so soothing. His hand caressing her cheek felt so gentle.

"It wasn't anyone's fault, honey."

"I couldn't protect her," she said, choking back tears.

If Gabe thought that was a strange thing to say, he didn't comment. "Sometimes things just happen. And we don't have a damn bit of control over them."

He smiled at her ruefully. "Don't blame yourself for something you didn't cause."

She sucked in a breath, determined not to cry. "I don't. Most of the time. But Terence did." He hadn't said it in so many words. But he'd implied it in a thousand ways.

"He was wrong. And he was a bastard to make you feel that way. He should have been supporting you, not making you feel worse."

She looked at him, wanting so much to believe him.

"Is that why you divorced?"

"Partly. We stuck it out for several months." Until Terence made it clear he couldn't get past any of it. "Of course, it didn't help that he was having an affair with his therapist by then."

"That just proves he's a dumb-ass," Gabe said. "Any man who'd cheat on you has to be incredibly stupid."

That made her laugh, despite the grim story she'd told him. "Thanks."

He cupped her cheek with one hand. Looked deep into her eyes. His were dark brown and so full of warmth and compassion she could have drowned in them. Wanted to drown in them.

"Terence was a fool to let you go," he said, and kissed her.

"DO YOU HAVE a preference on the wine? What do you like, white, red or pink?" Lana asked Gabe as they walked through the grocery store.

"Whatever you want," he said. He knew as much about wine as a minnow. Though he drank it willingly whenever someone else wanted it, he liked beer better.

They were picking up something for dinner. Gabe had offered to grill some steaks. He didn't cook a lot, but he could grill. He'd asked Lana if she wanted to go out but she'd refused, saying she'd rather cook something at her place.

"What kind of steak do you like?" he asked her as they walked to the back of the store.

"New York strip," she said decisively.

"I figured you for a filet mignon kind of woman." Classy. Expensive.

"Not me. I don't like filets. They taste funny to me. Give me a strip any time."

She let him pick out a couple of good-looking strips and put them in the cart. He limped along with her as they headed to the wine section.

"Since we're having steaks, we'll have a red, but I don't know whether to get a Merlot or a Cabernet. Or maybe a Shiraz. What do you usually drink?"

"Beer," he said truthfully.

She'd picked up a bottle and was reading the label, but at that she turned to look at him. "Don't you like wine?"

"It's okay. I just don't drink it much. So you get the kind you like. It doesn't matter to me. I'll have a glass of whatever you pick."

"All right, if you're sure." She frowned at the bottle in her hand. "I wonder if this is any good."

"Hello, Lana," a man standing beside her said.

Great, Gabe thought. Allen Paxton.

"Randolph. Good to see you again."

"Allen, hi," Lana said. "What are you doing here?"

Gabe nodded at him, wondering that himself. The man had said he lived in Corpus Christi.

"Stopped to pick up a bottle of wine. I have a date with a woman who lives here."

"Oh, well it's nice to see you."

"That's an excellent wine, by the way, especially for the price," he said, gesturing at the bottle she held. "I heard you talking about it."

"Really? I haven't had it. I usually drink California wines."

"The Australian wines are a bargain right now."

"I've had a few, but not many. I couldn't decide between these two," she said, pointing to another bottle.

That's all it took. The two of them started discussing wine in earnest then. The bouquet of this, the nuance of that. And then, for crying out loud, they started discussing corks. A cork was a cork, wasn't it? Gabe stood there like a dummy while they chatted together like best buddies.

He had no reason to dislike Allen Paxton. Except that he was a doctor and had infinitely more in common with Lana than Gabe ever would. He watched the guy critically. Obviously, Gabe hadn't imagined that Paxton had the hots for Lana. He hadn't taken his eyes off her the whole time they'd been talking.

Gabe's cell phone rang so he moved away to answer it. Lana and Dr. Knows Every Damn Thing About Wine were still yakking away.

The caller was a prospective buyer, so Gabe made arrangements to show him the boat later that afternoon. A few minutes later he hung up and turned back and they were *still* talking. Good God, how much could you say about a stinking bottle of wine? "This is good" or "this sucks" ought to cover it.

Finally they agreed on two. You'd think they'd just made the most monumental decision of their lives.

"Thanks, Allen," Lana said, placing the bottles in the bottom of the cart. "I appreciate the help."

"Sure. Let me know what you think."

"I'll do that. Have fun," she said as he walked off with a wave and a nod at Gabe.

Gabe was jealous. Ridiculously, stupidly jealous over a conversation about wine, for crying out loud. He felt like a loser. *She's with you, not him,* he reminded himself. *And that's what matters.*

"I thought we could have salad and French bread. Do you want potatoes with the steaks, too?" Lana asked, beginning to push the cart again.

"I don't care. Pick what you want."

She stopped and looked at him. "Is something wrong?"

"No." He shrugged. "Not really. That call I took was from someone wanting to see the boat. I told him I'd show it to him in an hour. Why don't I take you back to your house and you can wait for me?"

"How long will it take to show it?" She started walking again.

"Depends. On whether he's really interested or just jerking me around."

"I could come with you."

"No."

She didn't say anything, just kept pushing the cart. He realized what his abrupt answer had sounded like the minute he saw the expression on her face. Damn, the last thing he'd wanted to do was to hurt her.

"You don't want to do that, Lana. It would just be boring for you." Not to mention, whatever the result was, he was likely to be in a bad mood.

"I didn't mean to interfere," she said. "I thought you might like some company, that's all." They had reached the vegetable aisle by now and she started picking up potatoes, studying them in great detail.

He tried to explain. "The problem is, I don't want to show it at all." Didn't want to show it, didn't want to sell it, didn't want to think about losing it. "Since I don't have a choice, I have to do it alone."

Potato in hand, she looked at him with a sad smile. "I understand."

"It's not you, Lana."

"I know." She laid a hand over his that rested on top of the cane and squeezed. "Trust me, I do understand. Some things you just have to do yourself."

They finished shopping, had an argument over who would pay for the wine—which he won—and then he dropped her off at her house. Lana didn't chatter on the way, letting him stew about what he was going to do. He kissed her goodbye and promised to come get her as soon as he finished at the marina.

Assuming the guy showed up, one of three things could happen. He could make a bad offer, a decent offer or no offer at all. Gabe knew which of the three he was supposed to hope for, but that didn't stop him from wishing it would be one of the other two. He knew it was futile, but he wasn't ready to give up the dream. Worse, he wasn't sure he ever would be.

CHAPTER TWELVE

"HOW DID IT GO?" Lana asked when she opened the door to Gabe late that afternoon.

"It didn't." He came inside and followed her to the kitchen. "The guy was a no-show." Although Gabe had realized nobody was coming after the first half hour, he'd hung around for a while just in case. He couldn't afford to miss a possible sale.

"Oh, Gabe, I'm sorry." She squeezed his arm comfortingly. "I can't believe someone would make an appointment and then not show up."

"Happens all the time. I'm beginning to wonder if I'm going to manage to sell *El Jugador,* period. Much less for a decent price."

"I'm sure you will," she said.

He shrugged, not wanting to talk about it anymore. He looked around the kitchen, noticing Lana had set the table and that the makings for salad were on the counter. "Why don't I get the grill ready?"

"All right. I'm going to microwave the potatoes and

then finish them up in the oven. I wasn't sure when you'd get back, so I thought I'd do them the fast way."

One thing he really liked about Lana was that he didn't have to spell everything out. A lot of women wouldn't have let go of the topic that easily.

He went outside and cleaned the grill, then coated it with nonstick spray. When he came back in a few minutes later he asked, "How do you like your steak cooked?"

"Medium rare."

"My kind of woman," he said with a smile. Lana had put the steaks out along with some seasonings, so he sprinkled the spices on them. "You must cook out a lot. That's a Cadillac of gas grills you've got there. It has every bell and whistle and then some."

She finished slicing tomatoes and tossed them in the salad bowl before looking at him. "No, I don't use it much. I grill chicken on it sometimes, but that's about all I use it for. I suppose I should barbecue more, but I don't usually think about it."

"Why do you have the fancy grill, then?" He glanced outside and added, "It's a beauty. It does everything but walk and talk."

A wry smile twisted her mouth. "I got most of the furniture and household things in the divorce settlement."

That smile said it all. "Including the grill. Let me guess, it was your ex's pride and joy."

Nodding, she pulled the potatoes from the microwave and transferred them to the oven. "He adored it. He would have slept with it if he could."

He laughed at that. "I can think of better things to sleep with."

She smiled again reminiscently. "I know it was petty of me, but I thought he was going to cry when he realized the grill was included in my share."

"From what you said, he was a jerk. Serves him right. Besides, I'll bet it cooks like a dream."

"I actually thought about letting him have it, but the day I moved out, his soon-to-be new wife came over. She said they needed it more than I did and she was sure I'd do the right thing. So naturally, I told her to forget it. Then she told me I was using the grill as a substitute for the husband whose interest I couldn't keep." She shrugged and started slicing mushrooms to add to the salad. "I felt like braining her with one of the tools."

"But you didn't."

"No, I had a better idea. I had the movers load up that puppy then and there. The porch of my new apartment was small, and the grill barely fit, but at that point, I didn't care. I'd have kept it if I'd had to put it in the living room." Her brow furrowed. "Do you think that's vindictive of me?"

Gabe laughed. "No more than either one of them deserved, it sounds like. The new wife must be a nasty number. I thought she was a therapist. That's cold, what she said to you."

Lana shrugged and tossed the salad. "She never liked me. We socialized some before their affair—at least, I think it was before. I always thought she had a thing for him. Turns out I was right." Gabe picked up the plate of steaks and Lana followed him outside.

They talked some more while they waited for the grill to heat, then he put the steaks on. His mind wasn't really on the conversation. He was still brooding about the boat and the no-show. And the fact that if he did sell it, he didn't know what he was going to do.

"Want to talk about it?" Lana asked softly, pulling him out of his thoughts.

"Talk about what?"

"What you're obviously thinking about. What you've been thinking about all night. Your boat."

"I wasn't exactly thinking about the boat. I was having a career crisis." He checked his watch. "The steaks are ready," he said, putting them on the plate to carry them inside.

"Still haven't thought of anything you want to do?" she asked sympathetically.

"Nope, not a clue," he said, trying to sound cheerful as they sat.

After they finished eating, they sat at the table and talked. Lana fiddled with her silverware, then looked at him and said, "Have you ever thought about teaching?"

"No." He laughed at that idea. "Teaching what?"

"History."

His bedroom, he remembered. She'd been in his bedroom and found his secret. "Just because I like history doesn't mean I could teach it. Besides, I never went to college, remember?"

"You could go back, get a degree, teach."

He stared at her. She was serious. Was she just trying to help or was there more to it than that? He hadn't thought Lana was the kind of woman who got involved with a man and immediately wanted to change him. Maybe he'd been wrong. "What part of 'I hated school' did you not understand?"

Being cooped up in a building day after day, not only to earn a degree but then to sentence himself to that torture for the rest of his working life? Trying to teach a love of history to a bunch of kids, most of whom would never voluntarily open a history book, much less read it. He'd lose his mind in the first month.

"I saw your books, Gabe. You obviously love history. I just thought you might—"

"Tell me something, Lana," he interrupted. "Have you ever gone out with anyone before me who didn't have a college degree?"

She looked confused. "What does that have to do with anything?"

"Answer the question."

She frowned, started to say something then shrugged. "No. But I still don't see—"

"I'm not going back to school. If that bothers you as much as it appears to, then maybe we'd better rethink this whole thing."

"Rethink—" She stared at him incredulously. "Are you dumping me?"

"Other way around, I'd say." He knew he was overreacting, but he couldn't seem to help it.

"You are. You're dumping me over something ridiculous. I don't believe this."

"I'm a fisherman. It's what I do. It's what I am. I'm not a teacher." He pushed away from the table, got up and grabbed his cane so he could get away. He'd have given anything to be able to stride right out the front door, but that wasn't possible. The best he could do was limp out.

"Gabe."

She'd followed him into the room. He looked at her, thinking how classy she was, even when she was upset.

"Earlier you said you loved me. Did you mean it?"

He'd almost forgotten he'd admitted that. God, she was pretty. And sexy. And sweet. He was a fool. "I wouldn't have said it if I hadn't meant it."

She crossed the room to him. Put her hand on his arm and looked into his eyes. "Then don't go. Stay with me. We'll talk about it."

What else could he do when she looked at him like that? "Okay." He went to the couch and sat. Lana sat beside him.

"I can't go back to school. It's just not in me. I don't want to teach. I don't want to be inside day after day, trying to force a bunch of kids to learn in spite of themselves."

"All right." Looking at him, she frowned. "It was only a suggestion, Gabe. That's all."

"I know. I shouldn't have gotten so bent out of shape, but—" He hesitated, then forced himself to finish the sentence. "I know I'm not the kind of guy you're used to being with. Hell, you were married to another doctor. You're used to doctors and lawyers. Like I said before, white-collar all the way. That's never going to be me."

Lana smiled, leaned over and kissed him. Her tongue slipped inside his mouth, stroked his slowly. A long, sweet kiss that made him want more.

She pulled back and looked at him. "I don't want you to be anyone other than who you are. I wanted to help because I—I care about you."

She cared about him. She didn't love him, but she cared about him. It was enough for now, but he had to wonder if she ever would love him.

"That's not what you wanted to hear, is it?"

He took her hand and kissed her fingers, then put his lips to her wrist. "It's a lot better than 'go away, I don't want to see you anymore.'"

"I do care about you, Gabe. A lot. But love…I just don't know."

"It's okay, Lana. Forget I said it." The last thing

he wanted was for his declaration to cause her stress. He wanted her to fall in love with him without feeling pressured.

"I don't want to forget it."

"I'd rather you forget it than let it make you uncomfortable with me."

"Knowing you love me makes me feel…special."

"Yeah?" He smiled and pulled her into his arms. "Then maybe I'd better tell you again. I love you, Lana McCoy," he said, and kissed her.

SUNDAY AFTERNOON, Lana drove to the clinic. She had decided that the way things were going with Gabe, there was a very good chance they would make love…probably even sooner than she'd thought. And when they did, she wanted to be prepared.

In a town the size of Aransas City she wasn't about to march into the drugstore and buy condoms or pick up a prescription for the birth control patch. The news would be all over town the instant she did. So she decided to raid the clinic instead. While she didn't mind people knowing she was dating Gabe and assuming whatever they wanted, she didn't want to advertise every detail of their relationship.

Especially at this point, when that relationship was so new. He'd said he loved her and she believed him.

Sighing, she riffled through the cabinet where the

samples were kept. How did she feel about that? About him? Obviously she trusted him or she wouldn't be contemplating making love with him. But love… After Terence had left her for another woman, she'd thought she was done with love. Finished with men. But she hadn't met Gabe then, hadn't gotten to know him.

Gabe was so sweet to her. So patient. Maybe she was in love with him. He was certainly always in her thoughts. In her dreams, too, she thought, remembering one from the night before that had left her aching when she woke up. In her dream she hadn't been wounded or scared. She'd been strong, confident. And she'd knocked his socks off.

But today was reality. She picked up a box of condoms and started looking for the birth control patch. She remembered seeing several samples of those, but for some reason she couldn't find them. Finally she located one and pulled it out.

"Thank God," a male voice said. "I thought you were working and I didn't want to have a guilty conscience for not working on the weekend."

Lana whirled around, dropping both boxes almost at her partner's feet. She put a hand on her rapidly beating heart and stared at Jay, who was holding his year-old son on his hip. "You scared me to death!"

"Sorry." He grinned and picked up the boxes, handing them to her. The baby made chortling sounds.

"I thought the kid and I made a lot of noise coming in, but I guess your mind was somewhere else."

Ridiculously she found herself blushing as she accepted the boxes. "I, uh, just stopped by for a minute. What are you doing here?" She stuffed both boxes in her purse, thanking God that Jay was too polite to comment.

"I came to catch up on my medical journals." He glanced down at his son. "Jason's going to take a nap. I hope," he added, eyes twinkling.

"Don't you read those at home?"

He laughed. "Three kids, remember? Besides, Mel's entire Girl Scout troop is at my house." He shuddered. "Fifteen ten-year-old girls, screaming and giggling, is a little more than I'm equipped to handle. I volunteered to take Jason and get out of their hair."

"Wise man," she said.

"Yep. I did go to medical school." They both laughed, then Jay said, "You realize you've made my wife very happy."

"How did I do that?"

"You're dating her brother. She thinks you're good for him."

Lana smiled. "Thanks, but it's the other way around. He's good for me."

"Glad to hear it. You seem happy. More so than when you first moved here."

"I am," she said, surprised at just how happy she

was. The baby grabbed her hair and, with difficulty, she pulled it away and gave him her finger instead.

"Watch out, everything goes in his mouth. And he has a couple of teeth now, so when he chomps down it hurts."

"I don't mind." He was a darling baby. All blond and plump, with gorgeous blue eyes and chubby cheeks. "Could I hold him?"

"Absolutely," he said, and handed the child to her.

The baby looked at her solemnly, then smiled like sunshine and babbled to her. Her heart melted. "He's a beautiful child, Jay."

"Thanks. Takes after his mother," he said proudly.

"He looks like both of you." And since both Jay and Gail were attractive people, so was the child.

Lana put him up on her shoulder and he snuggled against her happily. Oddly enough, it didn't make her sad to hold him. She'd wondered about that, especially given the recent news about her ex. It just made her a little wistful. Maybe someday, she thought. Someday she'd try again.

"Gabe had any luck selling his boat? He's been really closemouthed about it and Gail and Cat are going bonkers worrying about him."

"No. He's afraid he won't be able to." She patted Jason's back. "I'm worried about him, too. He's trying to pretend everything's okay, but I know how much that boat means to him. And how much he loves fishing."

"Yeah, he does. According to Gail, he's never wanted to do anything else." He shook his head. "It's a damn shame. Has he decided what he's going to do when he sells it?"

"Not yet."

Jay leaned back against the exam table and smiled. "I get the impression you're the only one he talks to at all. He's changed a lot since his accident. Used to be pretty much of an open book, but he's not anymore." He added with a laugh, "Drives his sisters nuts."

He hadn't been as open as he'd let people believe, she thought, remembering his story about Bella. "I think Jason's asleep. Does he always conk out that quickly?"

"Usually. Gail says he's the best baby she's ever seen, but she's a little prejudiced."

"With good reason, he's a doll. Did you bring his carrier? I can put him down if you want."

"Thanks. It's in my office."

She followed him in there and put the baby down. He shifted to get comfortable but didn't wake. She watched him for a moment, thinking how incredibly sweet he was.

"You ever think about having kids?" Jay asked.

"All the time. But it didn't work out that way," she said with a last glance at the sleeping child.

Jay winced. "Sorry. I didn't mean to pry."

"Don't worry about it. Well, I'll leave you to your journals."

"All right. I guess I don't have an excuse anymore since Jason's asleep," he said with a grin. "See you on Monday morning."

Lana didn't leave immediately but went to her office. She needed some time to think. Seeing Jay's baby, holding him, had crystallized something in her mind. She wanted a child. She would always mourn the child she'd lost, but she wanted to move forward now and not stay mired in the grief of the past.

And though he didn't know it, Gabe had played a large part in that realization. Because he was helping to set her free of her past. Gabe wanted her. And she wanted him, too. For the first time since she'd been raped, she believed it might be possible for her to have a normal life again.

CHAPTER THIRTEEN

GABE AND LANA saw each other every night that week. And while they didn't make love, they did kiss. A lot. But he didn't do anything more, didn't take it as far as they had that day at his house when he was lifting weights. True to his word, he was giving her time. Lana knew he wouldn't do anything else until she made the first move.

She wanted to. Her sexuality, dormant for so long, had awakened again. She was becoming more and more comfortable with the idea of making love with Gabe. More and more excited about it, rather than worried it wouldn't work out.

They did other things besides kiss. They talked about all sorts of things. He said he talked more to her than he'd ever talked to a woman. He never admitted it, but she had a feeling he'd been pretty much of a playboy before his accident. After Bella had done her number on him, he clearly hadn't trusted women.

Lana talked, too, telling him things she'd never

told anyone. The only thing she didn't talk to him about was the rape. Mistake or not, she didn't intend to. It was in her past. There was no reason to talk about it, no reason to chance ruining what they had together.

Gabe was late tonight, she realized. They were supposed to eat dinner at her house and then go to a movie in Port Aransas. A chick flick she'd talked him into seeing. He'd agreed on the condition that he got to choose the next one.

An hour later she was seriously beginning to worry when the doorbell rang. Peeking outside, she saw it was Gabe and opened the door. "What happened? Are you all right? I was getting worried."

"Sorry. I should have called." He limped inside as she closed the door behind him.

"I was afraid you weren't coming," she said. "Or that something bad had happened."

He'd gone to the couch and sat. He didn't look upset, exactly. More like…numb. He was staring straight ahead, not looking at her.

"I thought about it. I almost didn't." His eyes lifted to meet hers. "But I wanted to see you."

She sat beside him, pleased by that simple statement. "What's wrong, Gabe? Do you want to talk about it?"

"No." Wearily, he scrubbed a hand over his face. "Yeah." He was quiet a moment, as if gathering his thoughts together. "I was showing the boat. That's why I'm late. It was a last-minute deal so I didn't have a chance to call you."

"Did he like it?"

He nodded. "He made me an offer. A good one. One I couldn't refuse." He closed his eyes and sighed. "So I took it."

She reached for his hand and squeezed gently. "I wish I knew what to say." Congratulations obviously wasn't what he wanted to hear, but under the circumstances the offer was a good thing.

"Join the crowd." He laughed with no humor. "I should be glad. I was afraid I'd never sell *El Jugador*. I didn't know what I was going to do if I couldn't get a decent offer. No, I do know, I'd have sold it for a lousy offer, eventually. I wouldn't have had a choice. But now that it's actually happened..."

"It's all right to be sad about it. Anyone would be." He didn't speak, so she continued. "And don't you dare say it's not a big deal."

"It's a boat, Lana. Selling my boat shouldn't be the end of the world."

"You're right, it's not." She squeezed his hand again, harder this time. "But it is the end of a dream." She wanted so much to make him feel better, but she couldn't think of anything that would. "It's hard to lose a dream."

"Yeah. It pretty much sucks." He looked at her. "But you know all about that, don't you? You must think I'm pretty damn pathetic, whining about losing my boat when you lost so much more."

He was talking about her baby, but she didn't want to think about her loss. She wanted to help him deal with his. "I don't think you're pathetic at all."

He snorted as if he didn't believe her. "Why are you being so hard on yourself? Let yourself grieve, Gabe. It's all right to admit that you're sad about losing your boat." And losing his dream.

He turned away from her. If he could, she thought, he'd be up and pacing. But he didn't even have that relief. "I don't want to think about it at all."

He looked so dejected. She wanted more than anything to make the hurt go away. She put her arms around him and hugged him. Pulled his head down to hers and kissed him. "I'm sorry." She kissed him again. "I'm so sorry."

He kissed her back, a little rough, a little desperate. He wanted to forget and she wanted to be the one he lost himself in. His tongue thrust into her mouth, strong, sure, making it clear he desired her. His arms squeezed tight around her, pressing her against him until she felt as if she were melting into him. His strength didn't make her afraid. The longer they kissed, the hotter the fire inside her burned. He needed her, as much as she needed him.

She'd never felt more wanted, never felt less fragile in her life.

He jerked his mouth away from hers and moved

her away from him. "This isn't a good idea. I don't have the willpower to back off. Not tonight."

"Then don't."

His eyes darkened but he didn't reach for her. "What are you saying, Lana?"

She smiled and put her hand in his. "Make love to me, Gabe. Tonight."

SHE LED HIM to her bedroom. Gabe looked a little out of place there, standing beside her bed, so dark, so intensely masculine in such a feminine space. The bed was covered by a white comforter sprinkled with tiny lavender flowers. The shams were white and a mountain of small- and medium-size multicolored pillows spilled over the spread.

Despite the urge to shove everything onto the floor, she picked up each cushion and arranged it carefully on the window seat, then pulled the comforter back before looking at Gabe again.

"Are you nervous?" he asked, a smile flirting with his mouth.

She bit her lip, wishing she couldn't deny it. "Why, do I seem nervous?"

His smile widened. "Yeah." He tugged her close and kissed her, then held her with her cheek pressed against his chest and his hands stroking her back, comfortingly. She felt safe, warm, and judging by the hard length of him pressed against her, very much desired.

She wanted him. Needed him. Most of all, she trusted him.

They sat on the bed and she reached out to touch his cheek. He caught her hand and kissed her palm, watching her as he did so, moist, sensual kisses that made her tingle.

She sucked in a breath and put her other hand on his chest. His heart beat strongly beneath his soft cotton T-shirt. She spread her fingers, feeling the muscles, wanting to see him again without the shirt.

She tugged it out of his jeans. He reached for the bottom and helped her, pulling it up and over his head, tossing it on the floor.

"You have a funny look in your eyes," he said.

"Do I?" She laughed. "I was just thinking—" She spread her hands over his chest, feeling his nipples harden. "I like the way you look."

He smiled. "The feeling is very mutual."

She smoothed a palm down his flat abdomen, stopping at the waistband of his jeans. He sucked in a breath when she skimmed her hand down the denim covering his erection.

"Your turn," he said, his hands on the hem of her shirt, waiting for her to say something.

She didn't. Instead she simply raised her arms and let him slip it over her head, watched him toss it down beside his own shirt. He didn't reach for her immediately but instead he simply looked at her, his eyes dark and appreciative. Her nipples tightened under his scrutiny. She wanted him to touch her, wanted to touch him.

"You are one beautiful woman." He skimmed his hands over the lacy cups of her bra, then cupped her breasts more fully, sliding his fingers over her nipples, circling them until they stood out in stiff peaks. She arched her back, thrusting her breasts more fully into his hands.

He found the front clasp, but didn't open it, waiting for her reaction.

"Yes," she whispered.

He popped the clasp and spread the cups, slipped the bra off and pitched it aside. But he didn't touch her, not then. Instead he just looked at her, and she felt the heat of his gaze.

"Perfect," he breathed reverently, and looked into her eyes.

Lana smiled. "They're just...breasts. Nothing special," she said breathlessly as he filled his hands with them and caressed her.

"Oh, darlin', not from where I'm sitting." Her laugh turned to a choked sigh as he bent his head, slicked his tongue over one nipple, swirled it around, then sucked. He gave her other breast the same treatment, then pulled back to look at her.

His eyes darkened even more. "I've been thinking about making love to you for so long. About being with you. Like this." He rolled her nipples between his fingers and she shuddered with pleasure.

"I have, too," she managed to admit, stunned at the sensations on her bare skin.

She leaned forward and kissed him, slipping her tongue into his mouth, gave another shiver of pleasure as he returned it. They continued to kiss, tongues touching, flirting, tasting. Deep, soul-stirring kisses that had her body tightening, eager for more.

Her breath caught and she moaned and bit her lip as he plucked at her nipples. Finally he bent his head to capture her nipple again with his mouth. Traced it, swirled his tongue around it, and she felt it peak and harden even more. Sucking on it, he stroked her other breast.

He eased her onto the bed, settling down beside her. He didn't seem in any hurry, instead lavishing attention on her breasts. Soon he had her panting, her breasts so sensitized she wondered if it was possible to climax from him rubbing and sucking her breasts alone. Restlessly, she shifted, wanting more.

His hand slid down to her shorts. He cupped her, fondling her gently through the fabric. "Why don't we get rid of these," he murmured huskily. He unbuttoned, unzipped them and tugged both her panties and shorts down her legs. She had expected to feel vulnerable at this point, but she didn't. He was looking at her and smiling.

He kissed her, his hand sliding down between her legs. He stroked her, slid a finger inside her. She tensed, she couldn't help it. Because she knew this time it wouldn't end until he was inside her. Making love to her. She wanted that, wanted him, but part of her was still anxious.

He kissed her mouth, petted her, caressed her, murmured sweet things to her as he patiently aroused her again. Gradually she relaxed, then tensed in a different way as her arousal grew. She slid her hand down to his jeans, feeling his erection through the denim. "Take these off," she said.

"Whatever you want, darlin'."

Soon he was as naked as she, lying on his back in the middle of her bed. She stroked him. She hadn't seen a naked man in so long, she'd almost forgotten what a pleasure it could be. Especially when the man looked as good naked as Gabe did.

Gabe groaned and put his hand over hers. "You're killing me, honey. I'm not going to last two minutes if you keep doing that."

She smiled, enjoying the feeling of power. The knowledge that she could affect him so strongly. That he wanted her and she wanted him.

Indulging herself, she slipped her hands over solid muscles, rippling skin, then lay on top of him as she kissed him until she thought she'd die if he didn't come inside her.

She helped him lift her up, straddling him, gasping in helpless desire as he filled her. It was a shock at first, but he didn't move, letting her adjust. Their eyes locked, she could see the effort he was making to let her control the pace.

Soon, she grew accustomed to him, loving the feel of him inside her, and she started to move. She sat up and her head dropped forward and she closed her eyes in pleasure, in abandon. He cradled her breasts as she rocked against him, squeezing her muscles tight.

"Lana, open your eyes." When she did, he looked deep into hers. "I want you," he said. "So much."

"I want you, too," she gasped, barely able to think. His hands slipped lower to hold her hips, to move her as he moved, to hold her tight as he gently thrust against her. She gave herself up to the pleasure, sliding up and down, the friction growing stronger, the heat more intense. Endless moments later, she came in a long, shattering burst of joy, and felt him follow her with a last, deep thrust, a guttural moan.

LANA LAY beside Gabe with her head pillowed on his chest and his hand lazily stroking her back and hip. She wanted to cry but she knew Gabe wouldn't understand, so she swallowed the lump in her throat.

He wouldn't believe her tears were from happiness, not sorrow. Their lovemaking had been everything she'd been hoping for and never thought she'd find again. Tender, passionate. Loving.

There had been no failure, no recriminations. No feelings of inadequacy. No reminders of the brutal incident. No knowledge that she'd let him down because of a past she couldn't control.

In fact, it had been perfect. At least, for her. She propped herself up on her arm and looked down at him. His eyes were closed and his mouth curved upward, as satisfied a look as she'd ever seen.

Relieved, she kissed his jaw. Moved to the corner of his mouth and kissed that, too. Then she traced a finger over his chest, down to the line of dark hair that bisected his abdomen and back up again.

"Gabe?"

"Hmm." He opened his eyes and smiled at her.

"Making love with you was very special to me."

"For me, too," he said. He pulled her head down, kissed her, and soon they made love again.

Afterward, as she lay there spent and more replete than she could remember being in years, she accepted, silently, what she'd been denying because it scared the hell out of her.

She wasn't unsure about her feelings. She had fallen in love with Gabe.

CHAPTER FOURTEEN

GOING BACK to work Monday morning was hard for Lana. It meant facing the real world after a weekend as idyllic as any she could remember. Still, she loved practicing medicine. How would she deal with it, if she suddenly couldn't be a doctor anymore?

She didn't even want to imagine it. She'd be miserable. Gabe was dealing with the loss of his career better than she would, she thought. If only he could find something else he could feel passionate about doing.

Over the next week they spent all their free time together. Gabe was working hard with his physical therapist, and Lana could see a lot of improvement in his range of motion. She wondered if and when he was scheduled for more surgery, but since he didn't volunteer the information, she didn't ask.

Lana was happier than she could remember being in years. She still hadn't told Gabe she loved him, even though she was more sure of that every day. Something held her back.

Because you haven't told him about your past.

Why spoil everything? she rationalized. She knew Gabe had a good idea of what had happened to her, so why tell him the details? He didn't need to know.

But the truth was, she was afraid to tell him.

"THE BAND IS GOOD," Lana said to Gabe Friday night. They'd met at the Scarlet Parrot and after dinner had gone to sit in the bar to listen to the music.

"Every once in a while Cam gets a decent one. You look like you want to dance."

"No, I don't care." She did, but she didn't want Gabe to feel bad, so she denied it.

"I don't dance much even without the bum leg."

"I don't, either," she said.

"But you like it, don't you?" he asked shrewdly.

She smiled. "Yes, but I haven't danced in years, so don't let it worry you." Terence hadn't liked to dance so she'd gotten out of the habit.

A man stopped by their table. "Hey, Randolph, how's it going?"

Gabe looked up at him. His eyes narrowed and he frowned. "Can't complain."

The man was blond and good-looking, with a deep tan that implied he worked—or played—outside. But Lana didn't care for the smirk on his face. "Heard you were selling your boat. Or trying. Tough break," he said.

Gabe shrugged. He didn't say anything, nor did he offer to introduce her.

The man turned to her with an appreciative look in his eyes and held out a hand. "Rod Winters."

"Lana McCoy." Not wanting to be rude, she shook hands, but he kept hold of it longer than she thought necessary.

"How about a dance?" he asked, adding, "Since Randolph's out of commission."

"Dream on," Gabe said before she could speak. "Get lost, Winters."

"Guess I'll make that a rain check." To Lana's surprise, he moved on, but not before winking at her.

"What was that about?" she asked Gabe.

He shrugged. "We go way back. Never could stand each other. He runs a charter fishing service, too."

"Why don't you like each other?"

"It started in high school over some girl we both dated, I think." He laughed. "It's been so long I can't really remember. Most recently he doesn't like me because a couple of his clients dumped him and decided to become my clients. He wasn't too happy about it."

"You were rude to him."

"He'll live." Gabe stared at her a minute. "What's wrong, did you want to dance with him? I can get him back over here if you do."

"No, of course not. But I would have turned him down more politely than you did."

Gabe grinned. "Yeah? Like you did me the first time we met?"

Lana gave him a dirty look. She'd forgotten about that. "Your brother is waving at you," she said. "I'm going to the ladies' room."

"I'll meet you at the bar," he said, wisely not adding anything to the grin he was already wearing.

LANA CAME OUT of the ladies room and walked down the narrow hallway toward the main room. As she passed the pay phone a man hung up and stepped directly into her path. She ran into him before she could stop.

"Well, now, this must be my lucky day," Rod Winters said. "Ready for that dance, gorgeous?"

"No, thanks." She tried to move past him but he took her arm to stop her.

"Don't run off, sweetheart. There's no hurry." His smile grew wider and he continued to hold her arm. "What's a classy woman like you doing with a loser like Randolph?"

She wrinkled her nose. He'd obviously been drinking before he got to the bar. "We're dating. Exclusively. So forget it," she said, finally losing patience. She jerked out of his grasp to walk away. As she moved past him, he followed.

"Hey, don't be so unfriendly. At least let me buy you a drink."

"Not interested," she said, continuing toward the bar.

"Don't be like that." He kept pace with her as she

walked. "Come on, baby, we'll get to know each other over a drink. You're the prettiest thing I've seen in a month."

She stopped a short distance away from the bar. "Are you deaf or just stupid? I said no, so back off."

"Your loss. Bitch," he added before he finally left her alone.

Bitch. Lana shuddered at the memories the word evoked. As she walked toward Gabe she fought for control. She didn't want Gabe to see how upset that simple encounter had made her.

"Was Winters hassling you?" Gabe asked her when she reached his side.

"Yes. But I handled it. Hi, Cam."

"Hey, Lana." He jerked his head toward Winters and lifted an eyebrow. "Say the word and I'll throw the turkey out. Never could stand the guy."

She glanced at the man, barely controlling another shudder. "No, I think he got the picture."

"I wouldn't count on it," Gabe said when Winters raised his glass to Lana and gave her a cocky salute. "He doesn't give up easy."

"Ignore him," Lana said. "I plan to." She wouldn't let a drunk ruin her evening.

Cam left them to serve someone. Gabe was staring at the man, and he didn't look happy.

"What's wrong?" she asked.

He frowned, still looking at him. "I don't like him hassling you. Not too long ago I would have let him know that. But now..." He shook his head. "Forget it. But I can still get Cam to throw him out."

She looked at him a moment before it dawned on her. He wanted to protect her and it hurt his pride that he couldn't. "Gabe, it's not a big deal. But I appreciate the thought."

He finally looked at her and smiled, cynically. "Yeah, I'm big on thought and a little lacking in the action department lately."

She didn't want to upset him further, so she made light of the situation. "It's not a crime to try to pick someone up. And being a jerk is no crime, either." She patted his arm, then leaned forward to kiss him lightly on the mouth. "It's nothing, Gabe. Don't let him get to you." Like he'd gotten to her.

GABE AND LANA left the bar a while later. Winters, thank goodness, had left before them. As they walked through the lighted parking lot, Lana made a conscious effort not to put her hand in her pocket. It was habit, she knew, not real fear that had her always reaching for her pepper spray.

Someday, she thought, she might even be able to look at a parking lot like others did. To see it simply as a place to park a car and not a nightmare of fear and terror.

"It's a beautiful night," she said. It was clear and warm, not as humid as summer nights usually were in Aransas City.

"Yeah, there's a breeze. Good fishing weather," Gabe said.

"Did you fish a lot at night?"

"Sometimes. Cam and I used to go and spend the night out on the bay. Drink beer, catch fish."

His voice didn't sound any different, but she knew he was wondering if he'd ever fish at night again. She wished she hadn't brought it up, especially when she heard his next words.

"Looks like the sale's going to go through on the boat. Closing's set for Tuesday morning."

"Oh, Gabe. I'm not sure whether to say congratulations or I'm sorry."

He stopped and took her hand, toyed with her fingers and smiled at her ruefully. "I'm not sure, either."

A man stepped out of the shadows and stood in front of them, blocking their way.

"Well, well," he drawled. "Fancy meeting you two here." His words were slurred and she could smell whiskey from a distance.

"What do you want, Winters?" Gabe said, dropping her hand and turning to face him.

Winters looked Lana up and down in a way that made her uncomfortable. "Thought the lady here might want one last chance with a real man."

Lana's stomach sank as she shrank back against Gabe. She didn't want another confrontation, but he seemed intent on forcing one. And she could feel the tension radiating from Gabe in waves.

"A real man? Give me a break. You're drunk, Winters. Get lost. She's not interested in anything you have to say."

"I say she is. Aren't you, darlin'? What do you say we get rid of the gimp and you and me will have us a good time."

Gabe took a step forward. Winters lashed out with his fist and Gabe staggered and swore, nearly going to the ground. But he recovered and lunged for Winters. Lana watched horrified, as the two men struggled. And then she saw it. Winters had—oh, God, Winters had a knife. A knife he used to send Gabe to the ground.

The blood roared in her ears, her head spun as she tumbled headlong into the past…

LIGHTNING FLASHED in the still, hot night. Large, jagged tears of it, with thunder booming in sharp cracks. Eerie, because other than the thunder, the storm seemed subdued. It started to rain, lightly at first then growing heavier, raising the humidity to unbearable levels. She walked fast, because she'd forgotten to bring a rain jacket. It was dark, dark as pitch.

The lights were out in the lot again and Lana hurried, wishing she'd waited and asked a security guard to walk with her. She looked around but didn't see a soul. She'd made this walk a thousand times. There was nothing to be nervous about.

The rain and lightning slacked off for a moment and she thought she heard the echo of footsteps behind her. She turned and looked around carefully, but still didn't see anything. Yet she sensed something. A presence. A threatening presence. She tried to shake off the uneasiness, telling herself she was imagining the threat.

More than a little spooked now, she reached her car and breathed a sigh of relief. She pulled her key ring out of her pocket to unlock the door and something hit her hard on the arm. Dropping her keys, she cried out and spun around.

Lightning flashed again across the sky, illuminating the knife blade glinting in a man's upraised hand. His smile glittering just as cruelly.

"Here, take my purse," she said, yanking it off her shoulder and thrusting it toward him. "There's not much in it but there's a little cash—"

He laughed and the sound chilled her to the bone. "I'm not after your money, bitch."

She knew what he wanted. Oh, God, she knew. And his hands reached for her, jerked her against him.

"Don't fight me, bitch," he whispered, his voice gleeful with malice. "I'll carve that pretty face like a pumpkin if you fight me."

My baby, she thought. *Oh, God, don't hurt my baby.* Fear, for herself and more, for her unborn child, paralyzed her. He held the blade pressed against her throat, nicking the skin and releasing a satisfied grunt from him as he did it. Blood, warm and wet, trickled down her neck. She heard his voice again as he dragged her behind some bushes, whispering obscene things, amused…aroused. She smelled his fetid breath and her stomach rolled.

"Get on the ground."

"No."

"You wanna die, blondie?" He pressed the knife harder against her throat, tightened his arm around her until she could barely breathe. "I said, get on the ground."

She twisted out of his grasp and stared at him, at the knife that was already wet with her blood.

FROM A DISTANCE she heard someone saying her name. Over and over, muffled then growing stronger. She blinked, shook herself. Gabe. What had happened to him? The man had used the knife on him. She'd seen him go down.

Then she saw Winters leering at her. He took a step toward her, his smile evil.

"No!" she shouted. She gave a bloodcurdling scream and sprang for him, going for his knife hand, raised and at the top of the arc.

The knife glinted cruelly, it was all she saw. She turned sideways, grabbing his arm and using his own momentum to bring that deadly hand down and drive the knife into his own leg. Jabbing an elbow into his nose, she twisted, levered him across her body and threw him on the ground.

Then she reached into her pocket to pull out her pepper spray, had it aimed and ready to shoot when she hesitated. Her attacker was on the ground whimpering, cursing, but unable to get up. The knife was nowhere in sight. He must have dropped it after she'd forced him to stab himself and he'd he hit the ground. She'd done it, she'd saved herself.

Then reaction set in. The attack had taken place in the space of seconds. She'd acted on the instincts that had been drilled into her in the self-defense classes she'd taken as soon as she was physically capable after the rape. *Go on the offensive before he can get to you. Be quick and be deadly, don't give him a chance to hurt you. Don't give him the chance to rape, or worse, kill.*

She sucked in a shaky breath, staring down at the man, willing herself to calm. Her heart rate sprinted madly, her breath came in shuddering gasps. She curved her arm around her stomach, striving not to be sick.

Again, she heard her name being called. She was safe. But Gabe wasn't.

She whirled and rushed to him, where he sprawled on the ground, cursing. She meant to help him, but instead she sank in a heap down to the ground beside him. "Gabe, oh, God, are you all right? How badly did he cut you?"

"I'm fine." His arm came around her, pulled her tight against him. "Are you hurt? Tell me, baby." He crooned soothing words in her ear as he held her. Comforting her, protecting her. She turned her face into his shoulder and wept.

"ARE YOU HURT? Answer me, Lana. Are you hurt?" Gabe would have given anything to be able to beat Winters to a pulp, but Lana needed him. He'd had to repeat her name five times before she'd finally answered. She'd thought he was hurt, when she was the one— Oh, God, what had it done to her to have this happen in a parking lot? When she could barely stand being in one as it was.

"I'm...okay," she whispered, her voice shaky. "He...he didn't hurt me."

A couple had just come out of the restaurant and hurried toward them. "Oh, good Lord. What happened here?" the woman asked as they reached them. She crouched beside them, her face concerned. "Did that man over there try to mug you?"

"Me? That's a joke. That bitch tried to kill me," Winters said, holding his hand to his bloody nose. He was sitting up now, instead of lying on the ground. "She assaulted me. Call the cops."

"Yeah, do that," Gabe said. "You're scum, Winters. I always knew it, I just didn't realize you were a total bottom feeder."

"I'm calling 9-1-1," the woman said, rising and

pulling her cell phone out of her purse. "Jim, you help these people up while I call. Then I'm going back inside the restaurant and get some help so that other one doesn't escape before the police get here."

"Escape? What the hell is this? I think she broke my nose, for no goddamn reason," Winters protested.

"Tell that to the cops," the woman's husband said, taking in the scene. "He's not going anywhere anytime soon," he told his wife. "Looks like the lady took care of that, dear. You go on and bring some help back."

Gabe narrowed his eyes and glared at Winters, who looked as though he'd gone three rounds with Evander Holyfield. Gabe had watched in shock, and not a little awe, as Lana went after the son of a bitch. He'd never seen anything like it, and he'd seen a lot of fights, broken them up, too.

"He had a knife," Lana said. "We need to look for the knife. It's evidence."

Gabe stared at her. Winters hadn't had a knife. Why did she think he'd had a knife unless… Oh, God, no. The bastard who raped her must have used a knife.

"It's all right, Lana. We'll take care of it." He pulled her back into his arms and prayed the police would get here soon.

CHAPTER FIFTEEN

GABE HEARD the sirens. "The cops are here," he said to Lana. She didn't answer. A few moments later Maggie Barnes got out of her cruiser and strode up to them. "We got a report of a mugging. What happened here?"

Everyone, including the Good Samaritan couple, tried to tell her at once. Everyone except Lana, who was still huddled in his embrace, not saying a word.

"That bitch broke my nose and maybe my arm, too," Winters said loudly, adding a string of curses. "I want her charged with assault!"

Maggie jerked her head at the other officer who'd just arrived. "Why don't you take his statement? I'll talk to Gabe and Lana."

Of course the sound of sirens had brought people out of the restaurant and there was now a sizable crowd milling around. "You all go back inside," Maggie said, raising her voice. "This is police business and we don't need a lot of onlookers."

"I'm not leaving," Cam said. "Delilah, can you handle the restaurant? Gabe's hurt."

"I'm not hurt." But Lana...He didn't think she was physically injured, but what was going on in her head? She looked as though she was in shock.

A short time later Delilah had herded everyone back inside, leaving the two officers, Cam, Gabe, Lana and Winters in the parking lot.

Winters was still cursing and complaining. Maggie walked over to him and spoke to him for a little while, then Gabe heard her say something about public drunkenness. The second officer helped Winters to his feet and took him to the police car. They drove off and Maggie came back and squatted beside Gabe and Lana.

Lana was calm. Unnaturally calm. She'd drawn away from him and was staring straight ahead. At what, Gabe didn't know. But her eyes looked empty. Broken.

"What happened here?" Maggie asked again. "Winters says Lana attacked him without provocation."

"Bullshit. He's a liar. There was plenty of provocation. Winters was drunk," Gabe said. "He met Lana earlier and hassled her and we both told him to get lost. We thought he had, but when we walked through the parking lot, he was waiting for us. He came up to us, punched me and then went after Lana. She didn't do anything but defend herself."

"He hit you? Are you saying he assaulted you?"

Gabe shrugged. "He hit me, yeah. That's not important. It's what he did to Lana that's important."

"Lana, is this true?" Maggie looked at Lana. "Did Winters verbally or physically threaten you? Or Gabe?"

"I—yes, he did." Her calm was starting to unravel. She looked shaken. "He—I thought he'd killed Gabe. Or hurt him badly. He was going to—I saw it. He...he had a knife." Her eyes went to Gabe, beseeching. "Didn't he?"

Gabe felt sick. Had she had a flashback? Is that what the whole thing with the knife was about? Had she just relived the previous attack? He took her hand, held it. "I don't think so, honey," he said gently.

"I thought—but I saw it," she insisted. "He stabbed you. He cut me. Here." She touched her hand to her neck. "He said he'd carve—" She broke off as she pulled her hand away and stared at it. "The blood," she whispered. "There's no...blood." She looked at Gabe then, her expression increasingly bewildered as she realized Gabe didn't have a mark on him.

To Maggie he said, "What the hell difference does it make? She thought he was armed, you heard her say it. The bastard attacked her and she fought back. I heard you tell that cop to book him on public drunkenness. You ought to be charging him with assault. Why are you hassling us?"

Maggie rose. "Lana, I'd like you to come down to the station and let me interview you. There's obviously more to the story than we can get in to here."

"Come down to the station? Are you crazy? She's going home. She's had enough without adding a visit to the police station."

"Gabe." Cam put his hand on his arm. "Come on, I'll take you down there so you can be with her."

"No. Absolutely not. The only place Lana's going is home to bed."

Maggie ignored him. "Lana, if you don't come voluntarily, I'll be forced to take you into custody. I don't want to do that. I really don't, but I'll have no choice."

"You're charging Lana?" Gabe asked incredulously. "For defending herself from a drunk who assaulted her?"

"The fact is, Lana assaulted Winters. His nose might be broken. Or his arm. I don't know whether it was self-defense or what exactly happened at this point. I don't want to charge her with anything," Maggie added. "That's why I need to interview her. To get to the bottom of this."

"I'll come to the station," Lana said before Gabe could answer. "Just…let me go, Gabe. Maggie's right. We can't talk here."

"If you're sure that's what you want."

"I have to. You heard Maggie."

He turned to Maggie and said quietly, "If you charge her with anything I'll charge you with police brutality and anything else I can think of."

Anger flared in Maggie's eyes. "Don't start with

me, Gabe. You seem to forget, Lana's my friend, too. I'm going to do the best I can for her." She took Lana's arm and helped her up. "Cam, why don't you bring both of them down to the station? Lana will do better with you and Gabe than in the cruiser."

Gabe didn't speak. He was too damn angry to say anything.

MAGGIE TOOK THEM to an interview room at the station. Before doing some preliminary paperwork, she'd found an ice pack and some over-the-counter pain reliever for Gabe. He had his leg propped up on a chair with the pack on his knee. It throbbed like a bitch and he tried to ignore the pain, but he wasn't having much success. He wondered how much harm the fall had done.

His leg wasn't the only thing hurting. He'd never in his life felt so helpless and useless than he had tonight. It wasn't an experience he was anxious to repeat. But if it had been bad for him, what had it done to Lana?

He looked at her and frowned. From her demeanor, he couldn't tell that anything unusual had happened. She was calm again. Collected. Almost too much so. She sipped the coffee Maggie had brought them. Only the fact that her hand shook as she set the mug down, indicated she was still reacting to the attack. But her eyes had lost that empty, bewildered expression she'd worn when she'd talked to Maggie in the parking lot.

"You really shouldn't be here, Gabe," Maggie said. "But since Lana asked for you to stay, I'm going to allow it. I have to ask you to be quiet while I interview her, though, unless I direct a question to you specifically. Do you understand?"

"Yeah, I get it. Keep my mouth shut unless spoken to. Does she need a lawyer?"

"Not at this point, no. Not until and unless she's actually charged with a crime." She opened her notebook and took out a pen. "All right, Lana, why don't you tell me what happened tonight?"

Gabe took her hand and squeezed it, offering wordless support.

"He stopped by our table in the restaurant," Lana said slowly, speaking for the first time since they'd come into the station. "Gabe didn't introduce us, but he introduced himself." She looked at Gabe, then back at Maggie. "He tried to pick me up when I was coming out of the rest room. I said no. I…thought that was the end of it."

"Then what happened?" Maggie prompted.

"When we went to the parking lot, he was…waiting for us."

"Did he threaten you?"

"I—" Lana hesitated, shook her head. "He said something, something rude to Gabe. Then he tried to get me to go with him again. Gabe told him to leave. That's when he hit Gabe. He—I thought he had a knife. Gabe went down and I thought he—I thought the man stabbed Gabe. And then he…he came at me."

"He denies attacking you, says he was just talking to you when you suddenly attacked *him.* Without provocation. Do you deny attacking him?"

"No. I thought he had a knife," Lana said again, pulling her hand from Gabe's and folding her hands together on the table in front of her. Carefully, as if the action would help her somehow. "Like…like before." She was looking down at her hands, not at either of them. Her voice was low, shaky.

"He attacked you before the incident tonight?" Maggie asked.

"Not…him."

"Goddammit, Maggie, Lana shouldn't have to go through this. Can't you see what it's doing to her?" The words exploded out of him, regardless of his promise to keep quiet.

Maggie shot him a warning glance, then turned back to Lana. "What happened before?"

She looked at Gabe for a long moment. "Tell her," he said hoarsely. "You have to tell her, Lana."

Her voice low and toneless, her face expressionless, her eyes locked on his, she spoke haltingly. "I was raped at knife point. Two years ago, in L.A. In…in the doctors' parking lot at the hospital."

"I'm sorry, Lana. So sorry." Maggie reached for her hand and squeezed it. "Did you report it?"

She nodded, looking at Maggie now. "Yes. I

couldn't describe him very well. He…wore a mask. A ski mask. They didn't find him that night, but they picked him up later." She swallowed visibly. "The case went to trial but he got off on a technicality."

"Damn. I'm sorry, Lana," Maggie said again.

She nodded. "I—I have a hard time in parking lots. I took self-defense classes after I was raped. They teach you to…act first."

Maggie didn't speak but she nodded and Lana went on.

"So when I felt threatened, I—" She spread her hands, helplessly. "I just reacted. I thought he was going to—hurt me, like he'd hurt Gabe. I thought he had a knife."

"Because Winters, that sorry son of a bitch, brought it all back to Lana tonight," Gabe said. "You're not charging her with anything. I want him put in jail. If you won't charge him with assaulting Lana, then do it because he attacked me."

"What exactly did he do to you, Gabe? You said he hit you. Was there more to it?"

"He slugged me and pushed me down. Then he went after Lana because he knew damn well I couldn't get up to help her. You don't have any way of knowing that he wasn't intent on harming her. If she hadn't taken care of him herself, there's no telling what he'd have done."

"I'm not sure I can charge him with assaulting either of you. He hit you, Gabe, but it wasn't really assault. And as far as I can tell, he never touched Lana before she went after him."

"So you can't do a thing to him, but you're charging Lana with assault. That is the most screwed-up thing I've ever heard."

"I didn't say that. Let me finish the interview and I'll tell you what is going to happen."

Gabe bit his lip while she took Lana through the rest of the questioning. Sometime later Maggie finished and stacked her papers together before standing. "Now I have to take this information to the D.A., and he decides whether to charge Lana or not."

"When will you know?" Lana asked.

"A couple of days at most. I can't say for sure what he'll do, but I can tell you if I were in his shoes, I wouldn't prosecute this case. Given your history and the fact that you believed your assailant was armed, I doubt he'll think it's worth his time to go to court. And even if he did, the judge could still throw it out."

"You're not…you're not putting me in jail?"

"No. I don't have to charge you if I interview you. The whole thing is now up to the D.A." She hesitated a moment. "Try not to worry. I know the D.A. and I seriously doubt he'll take this to court. But it wouldn't hurt to talk to your lawyer and tell him or her what happened."

"I don't have a lawyer here."

"I have the name of a good one in Corpus. I'll get

you her card." She passed by Gabe on the way out, put a hand on his shoulder and squeezed. "Take care of that leg, Gabe. You should see your doctor."

"I'm fine." He wasn't, but his leg was the least of his worries. He looked at Lana, who was sitting quietly, once again with a bewildered expression on her face. It hurt him to look at her, hurt him to think about what had happened.

Maggie looked at Lana. "Is there anyone you'd like me to call? A therapist, your counselor, someone like that?"

Lana shook her head. "No. No one."

"I'll be back in a minute with that information." After a worried glance at Lana, she went out.

"You need to go home. Let Cam take us home."

"I wasn't going to tell you. Even if I had, I wouldn't have chosen this way. But now…"

"You don't have to talk about it, Lana. I know what happened. You don't have to go into detail."

"You're wrong. I need to tell you about it. I should have told you before. But I just…couldn't."

"Lana—"

"Please, Gabe. I need to talk. But first, you're going to the hospital to have your leg looked at."

CHAPTER SIXTEEN

NO ARGUMENT could change Lana's mind about going to the hospital. Her mouth was firm as she pulled out her cell phone and punched in some numbers.

"Hi, Bill. It's Lana McCoy," she said, and gave Gabe's doctor a brief description of the accident. A few minutes later she hung up as Cam came into the room. "Dr. Black agrees you need an MRI and he wants to see you. He'll meet us at the hospital."

"I'll take you," Cam said. "Do you want me to take you home first, Lana?"

"Yeah, and you can leave me there, too," Gabe put in.

Both of them ignored him. "Thanks, but I'd rather go with him."

"I'm just glad you got him to agree to let you call his doctor," Cam said.

"He didn't," Lana returned with the ghost of a smile. "I called Dr. Black over his protests."

"Whatever works," his brother said, and put out a hand to help Gabe up.

It was obvious Lana would get no rest until he'd seen the doctor, so he gave in. Even though the last thing he wanted was to find out he'd screwed up his leg again. And he especially didn't want Lana having to take care of him. Not tonight, after what she'd been through. But with his brother and Lana ganging up on him, he didn't have much choice.

Besides, anything—even the hospital—was better than seeing that broken expression on her face. If worrying about his problems helped her forget hers, then that was okay with him.

They stopped at his house first to pick up his crutches. "Do you have any pain pills left?" Lana asked as Cam got out of the truck.

"No. I threw them out."

"We'll get some at the hospital, then."

"I don't need any damn drugs," Gabe said irritably. "I'm fine."

"Stop being so stubborn," Lana said as Cam went inside. "I know you're hurting."

He sighed and rubbed his temples. "Lana, I told you, I don't want to get dependent on the drugs. I can make do with aspirin."

She put her hand on his good leg. "One night won't make you dependent. Please, Gabe, let them give you something, just in case you really need it."

"Whatever," he said, abandoning the argument. He'd let the doctor prescribe them. Didn't mean he had to take them. No, he'd have to be hurting a lot more than he was now.

TWO HOURS LATER they were finally at Lana's house. Thankfully they'd managed to avoid seeing Winters, who had been taken to the same hospital. Neither he nor Lana needed to see the bastard again.

Since he couldn't stop her, Gabe let Lana get him settled on the couch with his leg propped on the table and his knee iced. But he drew the line at the drugs.

"I took aspirin. The doctor said I was all right, so quit worrying. It's you I'm worried about. You need to go to bed. It's late and you must be exhausted."

"I'll go to bed. After we've talked," she said, and went to the kitchen.

He heard her rustling around in there and wished he could get up and follow her. But he'd barely made it to the couch. He'd be pushing his luck to use his leg any more than he had to. He had no idea how long he'd be back on crutches, but at least the doc didn't think he'd done any new or permanent damage. Come Monday he'd be seeing the physical therapist and he had a feeling that meeting wouldn't be fun.

Not that his leg mattered. Lana mattered.

A few minutes later Lana came back into the room with coffee, for God's sake, just as if it was the end of an ordinary evening. She set the cups on the coffee table and sat beside him. "It's decaf, so it won't keep us up. Are you sure you're okay?" she asked him.

"Lana, give it a rest." He barely stopped himself from snapping at her.

He picked up his mug and drank some even though he thought drinking decaf was pointless. Coffee, in his opinion, should be strong, black and give you a jolt, otherwise, why bother? But if Lana made it for him, he'd drink dishwater.

Lana took a sip of hers, put it down, folded her hands in her lap and looked at him.

"You don't have to do this," Gabe said again.

She smiled, but sadly. "Gabe, you know I do. We have to talk about what happened to me. We can't just avoid it. Believe me, I've tried. I've spent two years trying to put it behind me, and when that didn't work I pretended it never happened. Look where that got me."

"I don't want you to have to relive that night again. You've already done it once tonight. Haven't you." It wasn't a question. He was almost certain she had.

"Yes, and I could have killed that man because of the flashback. I overreacted. It's just pure luck I didn't do worse to him."

"Blame Winters, not yourself. If he hadn't accosted you none—"

"They drill it into your head in self-defense classes. Be proactive. Get to him before he gets to you." She gave a humorless laugh. "Only I misjudged the situation."

"Don't do this to yourself, Lana."

She reached for his hand and took it. Looked at him earnestly. "Please let me tell you what happened."

He didn't say anything else, just nodded and waited for her to begin.

She put her hands together again and sucked in a deep breath. "It happened on a summer night, a little over two years ago. I worked in the same E.R. Jay did in Los Angeles. I had split a shift with another doctor because I didn't want to work late on the weekend. We—my husband and I—had plans. We'd been having problems and we were supposed to go out of town on a second honeymoon. To talk, reconnect. Be together." She laughed without humor. "We never made it.

"So it was late, about two in the morning. It was starting to storm. A lot of thunder and lightning but not much rain. The parking lot was usually lighted, but that night some of the lights were out. The one nearest my car was one of them. I should have—" She broke off, cleared her throat and started again. "I should have gotten security to walk me to my car when I realized that, but I didn't. I was in a hurry. I just wanted to go home. I didn't want to hassle with getting someone so, just this once, I didn't."

He frowned, not liking what he heard. "You sound like you're blaming yourself for what happened."

"No." She shook her head. "I'm just explaining.

But other people couldn't understand why I hadn't gotten security to go with me."

"What other people?"

"My husband, for one."

"He said that to you? Blamed *you?*"

"Not...not in so many words. But I know he thought it. I can't tell you the number of times he'd start a sentence with, 'If you'd only asked security...'" She pressed her lips together tightly. "I finally told him if he said it one more time I'd clock him."

He couldn't believe what he was hearing. Couldn't believe anyone—least of all her husband—would have tried to place the blame on Lana. "That's sick. It wasn't your fault, Lana."

She shrugged. "It was an error in judgment, and I paid for it. It doesn't matter. The point is, I didn't get help. The parking lot was deserted, except for me. As I neared my car I thought I heard footsteps. But I didn't see anyone, so I kept walking until I reached it.

"Something hit my arm and I dropped my keys. I turned around and there he was." She closed her eyes, then opened them. "I can still see him, perfectly clearly. He was about medium height, wearing dark clothes, and he wore a mask. A ski mask pulled down over his face," she said, and bit her lip before continuing.

"Even though I couldn't see his face, I could see his eyes. The lightning was intermittent but when it flashed it was bright enough to let me see. But anyway, his eyes…they glowed. With…malice. It sounds silly, but I remember thinking they were evil."

"That's not silly. What else would you call someone who preys on women?"

"You're right. He was evil." She was silent a moment, then continued. "When I offered him my purse, he just laughed. That's when I knew what he meant to do."

"Lana—"

"No, let me go on. He had a knife. He grabbed me, held the knife against my throat. Nicked it so I'd bleed. I felt the blood. It was warm, sticky, trickling down my neck. He told me he'd carve my face, like a—" she closed her eyes, then opened them "—like a pumpkin. Said he'd kill me if I fought him."

Gabe reached for her hand and held it. "I'm sorry. I'm so damn sorry, Lana." He wished for just five minutes alone with the bastard.

"I didn't fight him. I was scared to, you see. Because I was pregnant."

Oh, God, she'd been pregnant. With the child she later lost. Had the rape been the cause of her miscarriage?

"I thought I was protecting my baby. So I let him drag me off, behind some bushes. He told me to get on the ground. I said no, and he asked me if I wanted to die. So…I didn't resist. I just…let him. And then he raped me. He hit me. Kept hitting me the whole time he was raping me. Cursing me, hitting me.

"I was scared. So scared he'd kill me anyway, no matter what I did. It seemed like it took forever. I think he wanted me to fight back, but I didn't. I heard later he had used the knife on the women who resisted. He carved their faces, like he'd threatened me."

"You did the right thing. You're alive."

She looked at him and her eyes were bottomless wells of sorrow. She wasn't crying, but he wanted to. "I survived. But my baby didn't. I lost her anyway. I should have fought him. He wasn't very big. I might have been able to stop him. Or get away."

It just kept getting worse. How much was she supposed to endure? "Lana, for God's sake, he had a knife. He'd already cut you with it. He could have killed you if you'd resisted. You made the right decision. You're alive. No one blames you for not fighting him."

"Oh, yes." She nodded. "Someone did. My husband."

The pain on her face broke his heart. He gathered her close, though she resisted at first, he pulled her into his arms. "He was wrong, Lana. He couldn't have been more wrong."

She was stiff for a long moment, then she broke. She turned her face into his chest and wept. He just held her, stroked her back gently and added her ex-husband to his list of people he wanted to make pay for hurting her. A long while later she finally stopped sobbing.

She pulled back from him, straightened, wiped her face with her hands. Then she got up and walked into the bathroom. He heard her blowing her nose, splashing water on her face.

She came back carrying some tissues. "I need to finish. To tell you the rest of it."

Sitting down again, she took in a shaky breath and continued. "After he raped me, he left me there. On the ground, bleeding. He threatened to kill me if I told anyone. Said he'd hunt me down and kill me. At that point, I'm not sure I cared. I was already cramping. I think I knew, even then, that I would lose her. When I was sure he was gone, I got up and went back to the emergency room.

"I had them use a rape kit, and they called the police. Hospital security went out to look for him while the doctors worked on me. I went into labor, but the doctors managed to stop it. Security didn't find him, neither did the police, not that night. The police found him later. When he attacked another woman."

"I'm glad they caught the bastard," he said, then his stomach sank as he remembered what she'd said earlier. "Oh, God, no. You told Maggie he got off on a technicality."

"Yes, he did."

"I'm so sorry, Lana." Pitifully little he could say. Nothing he could do to ease her pain.

She looked at him and her eyes were hard. "Terence was sorry, too. Sorry it went to trial."

He stared at her for a minute. She was serious. Even after all she'd said about her ex, he was shocked. "Why?"

"Oh, he was happy enough they caught him, but he didn't want me to testify. He seemed to think I should just forget it. Pretend it never happened. I should put it behind me, he kept saying."

"I don't understand. Isn't that what you were trying to do?"

"He didn't see it that way. I think he was embarrassed. Embarrassed that everyone in the hospital knew what had happened. He worked there, too, and he didn't like the publicity."

"That's crazy."

"That was Terence," she said, and shrugged. "I didn't listen to him. I testified against that bastard because I didn't want him to ever hurt someone else. I sat in that courtroom and let the defense attorney rip me to shreds, make me feel like I was the one on trial. It was almost like being raped all over again." She looked at Gabe and shook her head sadly. "Maybe I should have listened to Terence. It was all pointless in the end. The rapist got off. I did it for nothing."

"Not nothing. Could you have lived with yourself if you hadn't testified?"

She looked surprised for a minute, then nodded slowly. "No, you're right. I couldn't have. I had to try. Even though the trial was—" She swallowed. "It was indescribably bad. But as bad as that all was, the worst was losing the baby."

"You said they stopped your labor."

"They did. That night they stopped it with medicine. They pumped so many drugs into me, but they did manage to stop it. Then a few weeks after the attack, I got an infection. I went into labor again. Nothing would stop it that time and they tried everything.

"I delivered my baby at eighteen weeks. She lived for a few moments, long enough to give me hope. But she was too small, too delicate. She—" Her voice broke but she went on. "She died in my arms. My doctor believed the infection was a result of the rape."

She broke down again, and again, he held her, rocked her, hurt for her. After she stopped, they were quiet a long time.

"Tonight brought it all back to you," he finally said. And he hadn't been able to do a damn thing to help her. She'd had to battle her demons and Winters by herself. Gabe should have protected her. Should have been the one she could count on, as she hadn't been able to do with her husband. But for his damn leg, he might have been able to prevent Winters from coming at her.

She pulled back and looked at him. "Yes. At first, when he moved toward me, I did get…confused. I did think I saw a knife. I did…remember that night. But then I came out of it. I realized he wasn't the rapist. I knew I was in a different place, a different time. But I still thought he had a knife. I fought back as I'd been trained to do. As I would have the first time if I'd known how."

"You shouldn't have had to," Gabe said harshly. "Winters probably wouldn't have accosted you if you hadn't been with me. He hates me and he knows I'm no physical match for him."

She put out her hand. Squeezed his. "Gabe, tonight wasn't your fault."

Great, now she was comforting him. "Lana, I'd give anything if you hadn't had to go through the attack. And if you hadn't had to relive the past tonight."

"Thank you." She put her hand to his face and smiled sadly. Her hand dropped and she sighed. "You knew, didn't you? Before tonight, I mean."

"That you'd been attacked?"

"You can say the word. I was raped."

He preferred the euphemism. "I figured it out. I suspected, the first time we went to dinner, and you pulled out the pepper spray in the parking lot."

"No one else ever picked up on that. I dated a few times right after the divorce before I decided to quit the whole scene. The men I went out with never noticed anything. Was it that obvious to you?"

"It was obvious something bad had happened in a parking lot. When I thought about what you'd told me, I was pretty sure I knew what had happened."

"And later you were certain." He simply nodded. "That's why you were so patient with me, wasn't it? When you wanted to make love and I kept freaking out."

"Don't make it sound like a hardship. It wasn't." He'd been patient because he loved her and because he'd suspected that she hadn't made love since the attack two years ago.

Suddenly everything made sense. All the hints she'd dropped about her ex. The counseling, his affair with the counselor. The son of a bitch she'd been married to had betrayed her with the counselor who was supposed to be helping him deal with his wife's rape.

Worse, the jerk hadn't made love to her after the rape, Gabe realized. If he had, maybe she wouldn't have been so scared, so reluctant to be intimate. Her husband's rejection, in addition to the attack and the loss of her baby must have made everything even worse for her.

He wanted to hold her. Comfort her. Protect her. "You need sleep."

"Will you stay with me?"

"There's no way I'm leaving you, Lana."

CHAPTER SEVENTEEN

GABE WATCHED from the bed as Lana went through her nightly ritual. She locked the doors, washed her face, changed into her nightgown. Rechecked the doors and windows one last time.

She came out of the bathroom looking so vulnerable, so fragile, it almost broke his heart. Not knowing what else to do, he smiled and held out his hand. "Come to bed, Lana. Let me hold you."

The smile she gave him was shaky but it was there. She turned the bedside light down low, climbed into bed with him and he wrapped his arms around her, holding her close to his heart. She smelled so good, sweet and sexy. Comfort, not sex, he told himself. He turned his thoughts away from lovemaking, knowing now wasn't the time.

She raised her face up to his and he kissed her. She returned it, her tongue seeking his, her hands sliding around his neck to pull him closer.

He kissed her again, then pulled back. "Lana—"

She put her fingers to his lips, her eyes big and solemn. "Kiss me. Make love to me, Gabe."

Oh, God, what was he supposed to do? He kissed her fingers, then held her hand. "Lana, are you sure this is what you want? You've been through so much tonight, maybe you should just let me hold you."

She sat up and stared at him. Her lip trembled and tears shone in her eyes. "You don't want me, do you? I told you what happened and now you don't—" Her voice broke. "You don't want me anymore."

"Oh, honey, that's not true. I want you so much it's killing me. Nothing could make me stop wanting you. It's just—" He stopped and swore softly, gently taking hold of her arms. "It's late. You're hurting and you're exhausted."

"It's because I told you. I knew I shouldn't have. If I'd never told you—"

He interrupted her by kissing her. "Lana, stop this. I already knew. I've known for weeks."

"But you didn't know the details. I wish I'd never told you."

"None of it makes a damn bit of difference in how I feel about you. And it sure as hell doesn't make me stop wanting you. But I'm worried about you. I can only imagine how hard tonight must have been for you."

She said nothing, just stared at him with big, sad, ocean-blue eyes.

"Are you sure?" he asked hoarsely.

Again, she didn't speak, she simply looked at him.

He lay on his side and pulled her into his arms, slowly, watching her all the while. He kissed her, as gently as he could. She returned it, sighing and nestling closer to him, her body warm against his.

Moving slowly, carefully, he caressed her breasts, first through the nightgown and then as she relaxed, he tossed the gown off. "You are so beautiful," he said, and teased her nipples with his mouth. They hardened immediately and so did he, even more. He sucked each one until she shifted restlessly.

"I want you so much," he whispered as his mouth trailed lower over her belly. "You can't imagine how much I want you." She arched her back and moaned, and he swept a hand down lower, slipped a finger inside her. She made a sexy sound that turned him hard as granite, made him want to plunge inside her right then, but he forced himself to slow down.

He'd always been careful with her, always tried to make sure she was getting pleasure from what he was doing. Tonight he mustered all the patience he could manage, waiting until he was sure she was ready, until she writhed and moaned, before he turned on his side and pulled her leg over his hip, then eased inside her. She was tight and wet, and she felt better than anything he could remember. He pushed forward and groaned, loving the feel of her around him.

She stiffened and put her hands on his shoulders.

He heard her suck in her breath, felt the tension

in that desirable body so close to his. "Lana," he gasped, looking into her face and kissing her mouth. "Stay with me, baby."

Eyes closed, she whimpered, a sound that froze his blood. "Open your eyes, Lana," he rasped. Her eyes opened and she stared at him.

He tried. Dammit, he tried with everything he had, but there was no possible way he could stop. The instant her soft, warm flesh gripped him, he'd been lost. But still, he tried again, pulling back from her with a groan but unable to leave her entirely.

"Don't stop. I—want you," she said, her arms encircling him, pulling him closer, tightening her feminine muscles until he thought he'd explode right then.

He thrust against her once, twice and came.

He pulled out the minute he could, held her and stroked a hand over her hair. "I'm sorry. I'm so sorry. I tried to stop but—"

"Gabe, it's all right. Don't...don't say you're sorry. Please. I wanted you to make love to me."

"No, you didn't." And it was anything but all right.

She kissed him. "I'm glad we made love, Gabe. I needed to."

He searched her eyes, still unsure he'd done the right thing. But it was over now and he couldn't change it. So he held her close, kissed her, tried to sleep. But sleep didn't come easily. The ache in his leg and the ache in his heart made it almost impossible. Finally he admitted defeat and got up to take a pain pill.

"I MADE COFFEE," Gabe said the next morning when Lana came into the kitchen.

"Thanks." She got a cup and sat across from him at the table. "How long have you been up?"

"A while."

"Your leg's hurting, isn't it?" She could see the lines around his mouth. "I shouldn't have—I should have let you go to sleep last night." But she'd been focused on her own pain, not his.

He reached for her hand and squeezed it. "I'm fine, Lana. I took a pill last night. I'm better this morning."

She didn't think he was, but she knew he would never admit it. The man was too stubborn.

"I need to go to the boat," he said after she'd opened the newspaper. "We're closing Tuesday and I want to make sure I've taken everything out."

"Do you want some company?"

He laughed without humor. "Trust me, you don't want to be around me today. Will you be all right alone? Why don't I ask Cat or Gail to come over? I'm sure they'd be happy to."

"You don't have to baby me, Gabe. I'll be fine." She wished he'd let her go with him. Let her comfort him, just as he had her the night before. "Maybe you should get Cam to help you," she said, worried he'd overdo it and cause even more pain to his leg.

"I'll be all right," he said. He framed her face in his hands, looking deeply into her eyes. "I love you, Lana." He kissed her and she clung to him a long moment. He pulled back and looked at her carefully. "Are you sure you're okay alone?"

"Yes. But don't you overdo it." She doubted he'd listen to her, but she had no choice but to watch him go.

LANA DIDN'T go to work Monday. She knew it was cowardly but she just couldn't face the firestorm of talk she knew the incident with Winters had caused. If she could avoid seeing anyone for another day, the fervor might die down at least a little.

Her doorbell rang around lunch time and her heart leaped, thinking it was Gabe. But when she answered the door she saw Maggie on her doorstep.

"Hi, come on in."

"Thanks," Maggie said, walking inside. She wore her uniform and held her hat in her hand. "Were you expecting someone?"

"Not really." She shut the door behind Maggie and they walked into the living room. "Why do you ask?"

Maggie studied her a moment. "You looked disappointed when you saw me."

"I'm sorry. I thought you were Gabe," she confessed.

Maggie looked down at her hat, then up at Lana. "I wish he was here. Do you want to call him?"

"Maggie, what is it?" She gestured at the couch. "Just sit down and tell me."

Maggie sat. "Are you sure you can't call Gabe?"

"He's with his physical therapist. I doubt it's a good meeting. I'm still afraid that fall the other night did more damage than they believed."

"I hope not," Maggie said.

"Me, too. Tell me what's going on."

"There's good news and bad news. I talked to the D.A. and gave him the information. After reviewing everything, he said he wouldn't pursue the case. In fact, he said it would be a waste of his time and the taxpayers' money, just as I suspected he would."

"I won't be charged? I won't have to go to court?" Relief swept through her.

"Not criminal court."

"I don't understand."

"Winters is furious that the D.A. threw out the charges. He says he's taking the case to civil court. He's almost certainly going to sue you, Lana. At least to recover the medical expenses, if not more."

Sue her? Civil court? How bad could that be? She had no idea, but at least it wouldn't be a criminal case. "You think he'll really do it?"

"I wouldn't be surprised. He's pissed about the way things turned out. Have you talked to a lawyer?"

"Yes. I touched base with Ramona Simon and told her I might be needing her help. She said to just give her a call when and if I needed her."

"That's good. Ramona's one of the best."

"Thanks for giving me her name." Lana felt as if none of this was real. What would she do if she had to go to court? Could she do it again? After her rapist had gone free she'd hoped never to set foot in a courtroom again.

She rubbed her temples. "Have you charged Winters for what he did to Gabe? As I said, we're not sure how much progress he lost because of that fall."

"I've charged him with harassment and public drunkeness. All Gabe has to do is show up in court. But that won't amount to much, I'm afraid."

Maggie studied her again. "So, how are you? The truth," she said before Lana answered.

"I'm...all right," Lana said, surprised to realize it was true. "I talked to Gabe Saturday night when we got home. He'd figured out what had happened to me but I'd never discussed it with him. I told him the whole story."

"Good."

"I'm not so sure about that."

Maggie looked concerned. "Why? What did Gabe say? Did he do something to upset you? I can see how much he cares about you."

"Oh, he was wonderful. Understanding. Compassionate. But—" She bit her lip, then shook her head. "Dammit, it's just not the kind of story you want to tell the man you're in love with."

"So you are in love with him. I wondered."

"I haven't wanted to admit it, even to myself. I was afraid of how he'd react when I told him about my past. Last time—" Lana stopped speaking.

Maggie cocked her head and considered Lana. "Was there someone else? Someone who didn't react the way you needed him to?"

Lana suspected there wasn't much that could shock Maggie—she was a cop. She took a deep breath. "My ex-husband couldn't deal with the rape. It broke up our marriage. He had an affair after I was raped, but the marriage was already over. The affair was just the death knell."

Maggie stared at her for a minute and then said something rude and crude that perfectly summed up Lana's feelings about her ex. She couldn't help laughing. "I knew I liked you."

Maggie grinned, then sobered. "You trusted Gabe enough to talk to him. That's good. Women need to talk about these things."

"You understand a lot. Is it because you're a cop or have you—" She stopped herself. "I'm sorry, I have no right to ask you such a personal question."

"Sure you do. We're friends, aren't we?"

"Yes."

"I haven't been raped, but when I was on the force in Dallas I was called to some rape crime scenes. One woman—" Looking at Lana, she hesitated, then shook her head and said, "She didn't survive. After that, I helped with self-defense classes."

Lana nodded. "I took my first course not too long after the attack. It was brutal, but it worked. I'm not the same woman I was before, in a lot of ways. Knowing self-defense had given me a sense of control."

"I have a black belt in Tae Kwon Do, so I know how you feel. We offer self-defense classes here, too, but we don't get many takers. I'm glad to say we don't have much violent crime in Aransas City."

"That's reassuring."

"Yes. Regardless of what happened last night, Aransas City is normally peaceful." She looked at her watch. "I have to get back to work in a minute. How is Gabe? He looked pretty battered Saturday night. I heard you made him go to the hospital. Good thing, if you ask me."

"His doctor says he's all right."

"But you don't think so," Maggie said. "Otherwise you wouldn't look so worried."

Lana shook her head. "No, I don't. I think he's anything but all right."

"Because of his leg? Or because of the boat?"

"Both. The boat sale goes through tomorrow. He went yesterday to make sure he'd taken everything out, and he wouldn't let anyone go with him. Not me, not Cam. No one."

"Maybe it was something he felt he had to do alone."

"That's what he said."

Maggie hesitated a moment, then said, "Lana, I don't want to be pushy but have you thought about seeing a counselor? Or joining a survivors group? I know there's a group that meets in Corpus. I could get the address for you."

"I had counseling in L.A., right after it happened." Her eyes met Maggie's and she gave her a wry smile. "That affair I mentioned my husband had? His counselor was the other woman. I had a hard time talking to my own counselor after that."

Maggie winced. "What a bitch. Guess that would be enough to turn you off of counseling for life."

"You're not kidding. And I went to a couple of group meetings, but they just weren't for me. Don't worry, Maggie. Last night aside, I'm doing okay."

"All right. But let me know if I can do anything to help."

LANA WENT BACK to work Tuesday morning with a heavy heart. Gabe had stayed with her every night since the incident in the parking lot. The night before, they'd made love. Awkwardly. She'd tensed, just for a moment, but it was enough. She and Gabe had even talked about it. Gabe had told her not to worry, that it wasn't surprising she'd be having a hard time after what had happened. He'd said he loved her and they would work it out.

Lana wondered if they really could. She hadn't dealt with her past. Not only had she broken a man's nose when he'd done nothing more than annoy her, but she wasn't doing very well with Gabe, either. How long would he want to try to make love to a woman who froze when he touched her?

She had told Gabe that the D.A. had declined to take the case to court, but she hadn't told him about Maggie's warning that Winters might file a civil suit. There'd be time enough to tell him if it actually happened. No sense in worrying him prematurely. She'd called Ramona Simon again, and the lawyer had agreed to represent her if she was needed. All Lana wanted to do now was to forget the whole thing, but that seemed impossible.

Her mood wasn't improved by the fact that everyone she saw, including her partners and office staff, had heard some version of the incident in the parking lot and most of them were wrong. The gossip hadn't died down, if anything it had spread like wildfire. Jay and Tim had heard the basic story from Maggie, though of course, they didn't know about Lana's past. And after they made sure she was all right, they didn't ask any more questions. She wished she could say the same for the rest of Aransas City.

She came perilously close to snapping at one of her patients when the woman conducted a ten-minute inquisition followed by a commentary about how violence never solved anything. After that, Lana decided to call it a day.

Walking into Jay's office she said, "Would you

mind covering for me for the rest of the day? I nearly brained Mrs. Berber a few minutes ago. If one more person asks me about Saturday night, I probably *will* brain him or her."

"Sure," he said, giving her a sympathetic smile. "That's one of the drawbacks to living in a small town. Nothing much happens so when something out of the ordinary does, the people talk. But don't worry, the gossip will die down soon. Especially if something else comes along to distract everyone."

She rubbed the back of her neck. "I hope so. I'm not sure how much more of this I can take. Thanks, Jay. I'll pay you back."

He waved a hand. "Not a problem. Go home, you look like you could use a rest."

But she didn't go home. Instead she went looking for Gabe. She knew he'd closed on the boat that morning and she hadn't heard from him since. His truck was in his driveway, so she used the key he'd given her to let herself in. She found him in the spare bedroom lifting weights.

"Hi," she said.

His only response was a grunt.

She watched him do leg curls for a moment, then said, "Are you sure you should be pushing yourself so hard? It can't be good for your leg."

He finished the set. "It was either lift weights or get drunk and I decided it was too early to get drunk yet."

"Does that mean you plan to later?"

"I don't know. Maybe." He started on another set. "Why are you off so early?"

"I couldn't stand answering the same questions about Saturday night over and over, so Jay said he'd cover for me. And I was worried about you."

"Me?" He laughed. "I'm just peachy, darlin'. I'm no longer broke. Of course, I still don't have a job, but hey, one thing at a time."

"You'll find something. You just haven't hit on what you want to do yet." She sat beside him on the bench. "Can I do something to help?"

"Yeah, you can move so I can do another set."

She ignored that comment. "Gabe, let me help."

"You can't. And I don't want to talk about it. Just leave me alone, Lana."

CHAPTER EIGHTEEN

SHE LOOKED hurt, and he cursed himself for his bluntness. He set down the bar and sat up. "I didn't mean that the way it sounded. It's just—I know you want to help, but there's nothing you can do, Lana."

"All right. But if you want to talk, I'm here."

She left a short time later after he agreed to come see her that evening. While he appreciated her offer, he wasn't going to whine about his employment problems to Lana. She didn't need that on top of what she was already dealing with.

He spent the following day looking at the classifieds in the employment section, picking up the paper and putting it back down countless times. Finally late that afternoon he forced himself to go through the ads more carefully. Not much choice for an out-of-work fishing captain.

Nothing much appealed to him. Problem was, it was damn hard to go from being your own boss to being under someone else's control, no matter how good a boss they might be. So he looked at the opportunities section, as well. The pickings were really slim there, especially for someone without a great deal of capital to invest and who wanted to stay in the Corpus/Aransas City area. Corpus Christi was only twenty to thirty minutes away, depending on how fast you drove.

Maybe he should buy the Laundromat that was for sale in Aransas City. He knew of it and thought it did a pretty good business. He closed his eyes and tried to imagine it. No, that wasn't going to work. He knew nothing about running a Laundromat and he didn't care enough to find out how.

Maybe Lana was right, and he should go back to school. Yeah, right. He'd been a poor student in high school, why should he be any better now? But what if he went to technical school? He could be a boat mechanic. Like most charter fishing captains, he knew a fair amount about fixing boats already. He'd just never thought about doing it for a living.

He was still thinking about it when he went to Lana's that evening. Another car stopped in front of her house and a man in a suit got out and walked up the steps. Gabe pulled into the driveway and got out, just in time to see Lana open the door. The man handed her a brown envelope, said something Gabe couldn't hear and turned around and left.

She was staring down at the envelope with an odd expression on her face when he reached her. "What was that about?"

Lana raised her gaze to his. "I've been served."

"Served what?"

"I haven't looked, but I have a bad feeling I know."

"What the—" He broke off as Lana shut the door, then opened the envelope and read the papers.

"Winters has filed a civil suit against me. He wants money to pay for medical expenses and loss of work due to his injuries."

"Dammit, he must have done it the minute he found out the D.A. dropped the charges against you."

"I guess he did. This says I have twenty days to file an answer."

"You don't seem surprised. Did you know this would happen? I should have, but I didn't think of it. It's exactly what Winters *would* do."

"Maggie warned me he'd been talking about it."

"You didn't mention any of this to me."

"I didn't want you to worry." She turned aside, tossed the papers on the coffee table and sat on the couch. "There was nothing either of us could do, so I didn't see the sense in your getting upset, too."

Nothing he could do. That sounded familiar. He couldn't help her with this, he couldn't help her with anything. He followed her to the couch and sat beside her.

"If I could get my hands on Winters—"

"Gabe, it's my responsibility. If I hadn't overreacted, none of this would be happening. For God's sake, I broke the man's nose."

"You were defending yourself, Lana."

"From a drunk, not a rapist."

"You didn't realize that at the time."

"It doesn't matter. At least I won't have to go to jail. Even if…even if I do have to go into a courtroom again." She bit her lip and looked away.

"What is it?"

She got up and paced the room before coming back and standing in front of him. "When I told you the story, I didn't talk much about the actual trial."

"No." She'd said it was bad, and the rapist had gotten off on a technicality, but that's all she'd mentioned. "You want to tell me now?"

She closed her eyes, then opened them. "I don't want to even think about it, but I don't have that choice. The trial was a media circus. It didn't start out that way, but by the time it was over it had even hit the national news."

"Why? Was he well known?"

"No, it had very little to do with him. There was a reporter who had problems with the hospital where I worked. He and the administrators didn't get along. He wanted to give the administrators and the hospital a bad reputation. Unfortunately, I got caught in the fallout."

"Great."

"Yes, he was ecstatic. That technicality I told you about? It was a little more than that. I just said that to avoid going into all the details."

"The hospital was at fault?"

"Technically, yes. The doctor who took the sample from me had another emergency roll in right after me. He had to step out of the room for a minute before the police took charge of the evidence to send it to the crime lab. That broke the chain of custody. So the results were disallowed and we had no DNA evidence to directly link the suspect to me. Which helped convince a jury to let him off. And since I never saw his face, they didn't believe I could positively identify him. Even though I knew it was him." She looked at Gabe grimly. "I recognized his voice. I testified to that, but it wasn't enough."

"God, Lana, I'm sorry. That must have been hell for you."

"Hell doesn't begin to describe it. The trial was in all the papers. Because of the hospital, not because of me. The reporter made it sound as if these things happened all the time at that hospital, which wasn't the case. And then when reporters learned that I was on staff there, they said the hospital couldn't even get it right for one of their own."

"Tell me they didn't release your name. I thought rape victims' identities were protected."

"Supposedly they are. My identity wasn't disclosed in the press, other than that I worked at the hospital, but everyone knew. That's one of the reasons I moved, you know. I was so tired of everyone knowing—or thinking they knew—everything about me. Speculating about me, about my marriage. It was too much."

"You're afraid if this goes to trial it will be another media circus."

"Do you blame me?"

"No, but Aransas City's awfully small. And this is a civil case, not a criminal one. I can't see that happening here." He was trying to reassure her, but he didn't think it was working.

"I hope you're right." She laughed without humor. "I didn't want to ever go into a courtroom again after my last experience. Way to blow that one, huh?"

He stroked a hand over her hair. "You didn't blow anything, honey. Try not to worry. It won't be like the last time."

She sighed and moved away from him. "I'm going to call my lawyer now. I hope she can make time for me soon."

He hoped the lawyer could ease her fears. But in the meantime, he had an idea that might just help her.

GABE PULLED UP outside Winters' place early the next morning and took a deep breath, steeling himself for the meeting to come. Winters wouldn't cave easily. And once he realized how much Gabe wanted him to drop the charges, he'd twist the knife in deep. Gabe had never imagined begging the man for anything, but if that's what it took, that's what he'd do.

The place was a dump, with garbage littering a

yard choked with weeds. The house hadn't seen new paint in years and what was left was flaked and peeled. The gravel drive needed more gravel and the truck that was parked in it could have used work, too. Gabe had heard that business hadn't been so good for Winters lately, and it looked as if the rumor was true.

Might as well get it over with. He limped up the broken walkway, glad that he'd been cleared for the cane again. He'd have gone down for sure using crutches. He rang the bell and waited.

Winters—a bandage on his nose and his arm in a sling—opened the door and stared at him. "What the hell do you want?"

Gabe didn't wait for an invitation. He stuck his cane in the door in case Winters tried to shut it in his face and limped inside. "I need to talk to you."

The inside wasn't much better than the outside. Newspapers lay scattered on the floor and it looked as if nobody had washed dishes in the last month, or even taken them to the kitchen.

Since his leg was killing him, he took a seat in the armchair. Much as he hated to put himself in a weak position so quickly, he didn't have a choice.

"Have a seat. Make yourself right at home," Winters said sarcastically. "What do you want, Randolph?"

He just said it, straight out. "I want you to drop the civil suit against Lana."

Winters stared at him incredulously for a minute then laughed. "Yeah, right. Funny."

"I'm serious."

"What you are is crazy. Don't waste your breath, loser. No way am I going to drop the case against that bitch. In case you didn't notice not only did she break my nose—" he pointed to the bandages on his face "—but check this out." With his good hand, he tapped his arm that rested in a sling. "I can't work with one arm."

"What's wrong with your arm?"

"You know what's wrong with it. That bitch you were with damn near broke it."

"But it's not broken." Trust Winters to play up a minor injury for all it was worth. He was surprised he wasn't wearing a neck brace.

"It could have been. The doctor said it was the worst sprain he'd ever seen."

Yeah, he believed that. "I'm asking you to drop the civil suit," Gabe repeated.

"Give me one good reason why I should."

"Because she doesn't deserve it."

Winters took a seat on his couch. Picked up a cigarette from the crumpled pack on the coffee table and lit it, blowing the smoke out with evident enjoyment. "She deserves everything she gets. She assaulted me for no reason. Look at my freaking nose. She did break that."

It gave Gabe a great deal of satisfaction to see the nose in question was still swollen beneath the tape. If Winters hadn't accosted Lana in the first place, he wouldn't have gotten what was coming to him. "Your lawyer must have explained the situation to you when the D.A. dropped the charges. Lana thought you had a knife. She was defending herself."

Winters' eyes narrowed as he squinted against the smoke. He leaned back and gave him a lazy smile, then sucked in more smoke. "Yeah, yeah. Tell it to the judge when I see her in court. For all I know, she made up that story about being attacked. Trying to cover her ass."

Gabe's lips tightened as he fought for control of his temper. "The case went to trial in Los Angeles. She didn't make it up. That was one of the things that persuaded the D.A. to drop the criminal charges."

Winters shrugged. "Even so, it's not my problem." He tapped his sprained arm. "My problem is I'll have to hire extra help and be off work a lot until this heals. And there's no telling how long until it does. I'm supposed to just let that go? Because you said 'pretty please'?" He laughed again. "I don't think so."

"I'll compensate you until you're recovered." Now that he'd sold the boat, he had money. Not that he wanted to give it to Winters, but if it kept Lana out of court, he'd be more than willing.

"I don't know." He pretended to consider it. Ground out his cigarette and lit another. "What about my pain and suffering? You gonna compensate me for that, too?"

Pain and suffering, his ass. Lana's pain and suffering was infinitely worse than Winters' could ever be. But he knew better than to say that.

"You don't know that you'll get anything if you pursue it. She'll testify she thought you were armed. And you came after her, anyway. Seems to me the sympathy would be toward her. You want to risk coming away with nothing?"

"The bitch assaulted me. I ought to get something out of that. And I shouldn't lose money because of what she did to me. No sir, I damn well shouldn't."

"Cut to the chase, Winters. What will it take to make this all go away?"

He considered him and smiled. "She's really got you whipped, doesn't she?"

"What will it take?" Gabe repeated, not taking the bait. Winters didn't understand what he had with Lana. Hell, Gabe wasn't sure he understood it, but he knew he'd do anything he had to, to make sure Lana didn't have to set foot in a courtroom again.

Winters crushed his cigarette out in the overflowing ashtray. Shot him a crafty look and said, "So you'll do whatever I want?"

"Yeah. Whatever you want."

"Anything at all, huh?" He rubbed his jaw, clearly enjoying himself. "Well, now, I've been thinking of expanding my operation. Another boat would be nice. Seems to me you have one for sale."

For once he was happy he'd closed the deal.

"Nope. I just sold *El Jugador.* Closed on it yesterday. It'll have to be something else."

"Too bad." He rubbed his jaw again. "You'll pay me?"

Gabe nodded. "Enough so you can hire someone to help until you're ready to work again." And God knew how long that would be since Winters was bound to milk this for all it was worth.

"And drop those bogus charges against me?"

"I can't drop the charges. That's up to the cops. But if I don't show up in court, they have no case. I'll do that, if you don't take Lana to civil court over this."

Winters leaned back and propped his feet on the coffee table. Rested his good hand on his stomach. "You still got your tackle? Or did you sell it with the boat?"

His fishing tackle. His stomach sank. He should have known Winters would want it, but he'd never even thought of it. Thousands of dollars worth of expensive equipment, rods, reels, belts, everything needed to run a charter service, accumulated over years of working.

If he gave all that to Winters he could kiss goodbye any chance of ever running a charter service again. He could never afford to replace both the boat and the equipment, not on the money he'd be likely to make.

But what choice did he have?

"I have it."

Winters smiled. "What's she worth to you, Randolph?" he asked softly. "Is she that good? Good enough you're willing to part with that tackle?"

Though he wanted to smash his fist into the man's face, Gabe ignored the provocative comment. "I'm willing. So is it a deal?"

Winters stared at him a long moment, then shrugged. "Yeah, it's a deal."

"Good. I have a few conditions."

"Conditions? Like what?"

"This deal stays between you and me. For all anyone knows, you just had an attack of decency and decided to let Lana off the hook."

Of course, no one who knew Winters would believe it, but as long as Lana didn't find out, Gabe didn't care. She'd have a fit if she discovered what he was doing.

"All right. What else?"

"You don't talk about the situation. You act like it never even happened. And you don't so much as look at Lana again, much less go near her."

"Say I agree, how do I know you'll keep your end of the deal?"

Gabe pulled out a checkbook and wrote him a check. "First payment. You can bring someone over to my place tomorrow to help you load the tackle." He tore the check out and held it. "But first, I want to hear you tell your lawyer to drop that suit."

Winters rolled his eyes but he picked up the phone and dialed a number. A short time later he looked at Gabe. "Okay, the suit's gone away."

Winters took the check and scanned it, then looked at Gabe. "You're crazy. No woman's worth all this."

"Lana is." It was worth anything he had to do to keep Lana out of court. He got up to leave. At the door, he paused. "One more thing, Winters. If I hear that you've so much as mentioned her name, you're a dead man."

"Oh, come on, Randolph. Don't you think that's a little melodramatic?"

"Is it? If I was you, I wouldn't push my luck and try to find out."

CHAPTER NINETEEN

FORTUNATELY, Ramona Simon was able to meet with Lana the next morning. After the meeting, she went back to work. Though she went through the motions, her mind was on the upcoming lawsuit, not on medicine. She shut herself in her office during the lunch hour and thought about her conversation with Ramona.

The lawyer had been encouraging. Lana had told her she would be happy to pay the man's medical expenses and compensate him for any work he missed, but she didn't want to have to go to court over it. Ramona said she'd see what she could do, that her offer to pay might well convince the man to drop the suit.

But would it? He seemed like a vindictive man and she'd not only injured him, she'd hurt his ego, as well. Still, maybe she was worrying for nothing. Even if he went through with it, a civil suit wouldn't necessarily generate a lot of publicity. Although, a case like this would be big news for Aransas City.

She could see the headlines now. Media coverage would be bound to unearth the earlier trial and all its publicity. Oh, God, she didn't want to go through that experience a second time. She had moved across the country to get away from it. She loved Aransas City, she didn't want to leave.

Guilt nagged her, as well. She'd hurt an unarmed man. But would she go back to the way she was before, when she couldn't defend herself? When she'd been at the mercy of a man wielding a knife?

No, she could never be that woman again. Didn't want to be, even if she could. She'd had no choice but to learn to defend herself. Yet defending herself was one thing. Having a flashback and hurting someone because of it was a whole other situation.

She had to find a better way to deal with her past trauma so that a situation like this wouldn't happen again. She put her hands to her temples and massaged them, not wanting to admit what she knew was the truth. She needed more therapy. Clearly, she hadn't healed as well as she'd thought she had. Trouble was, she wasn't ready to trust a therapist again.

Late that afternoon, as she was about to leave work, the receptionist buzzed her and told her Ramona was on the line. Surprised to hear from her so soon, she picked up. "Hi, Ramona. What's up?"

"I have good news. The suit has been dropped."

She was conscious of overwhelming relief. "Wow, when Maggie said you were good, she wasn't kidding."

"Afraid I can't take credit for this. I hadn't even made your offer yet and I was notified the suit had been dropped."

"That doesn't make sense. He just filed. Why would he drop it if you haven't told him I would pay his expenses?"

"No idea, but he did."

"I wonder if someone changed his mind for him."

"Talked him out of it, you mean? It's certainly possible. Maybe he realized the sympathy would likely have been for you as the victim of a violent crime in the past."

"You have to admit, it seems a little coincidental that he'd suddenly drop the case the day after I was served."

"Stranger things have happened," Ramona said. "I'm glad it worked out so easily for you."

"Yes, me, too." She would bet her last dollar that Gabe had been behind Winters dropping the lawsuit. She wondered what it had cost him. How much had Gabe paid him? Getting Gabe to tell her wouldn't be easy but she intended to force the issue.

LANA DECIDED to take Gabe by surprise and went directly to his house after work. She didn't beat around the bush, as soon as she walked in she confronted him.

"I got a call from my lawyer a few minutes ago."

He was sitting on the couch watching TV but at that he looked up. "How's she working out? Did you like her?"

"I liked her fine. She told me the plaintiff decided to drop the suit."

"Winters dropped it? That's great!" He paused and looked at her. "You don't look very happy."

She made an impatient gesture. "Of course I'm happy I won't have to go to court. But I want to know what you did to get Winters to drop it."

"Me? I didn't have anything to do with it. Why would you think I did? He must have decided on his own. Maybe his lawyer convinced him."

"Gabe, please tell me."

"Nothing to tell," he said firmly.

She didn't believe him for a moment. "Did you offer him money? Because if you did, I'm paying you back. I won't have you paying for what I did."

"Can we just forget this?"

"Not until you tell me the truth." Their gazes met and held. "You might as well tell me. I'll find out somehow, you know I will."

He swore, then shrugged. "Yeah, I paid him. I had money from the sale of the boat, so I figured, why not? It was worth it if he'd drop the suit, and it worked."

"I'm paying you back. Don't you dare argue with me."

"Fine. Now can we forget it?"

"Gabe, I appreciate what you did for me. But I can't let you pay for something that's my problem."

"Yeah, I got that. Can we for God's sake quit talking about this?"

She could tell he was really irritated so she did as he said. But she promised herself that first thing in the morning she would write him a check.

THE SOUND OF SCREAMS jerked Gabe out of a deep sleep. In the throes of a nightmare, Lana was thrashing around in the bed. Without thinking, he put his hands on her arms, trying to settle her.

"Lana, honey, wake up. You're dreaming."

"Stop it! Don't touch me!"

Big mistake, he thought when the heel of her hand smashed into his cheek. Wincing, he let go of her immediately and turned on the light. His eyes watered and he stifled a curse. By the grace of God, she'd missed his nose.

"Lana, wake up." He repeated her name until he finally got through to her.

Her eyes blinked open and she stared at him, panic still swimming in the depths of her eyes.

Slowly, the panic cleared. "Gabe?"

"It's me, baby. Shh, you're okay." He kissed her forehead. "You're safe now."

"I...was dreaming." She reached up and touched his injured cheek with gentle fingers. "Your cheek is red. It looks like... Did I do that?"

Their eyes met. He didn't know what to say. If he said no he'd done it to himself, she'd know it was a lie. "It's fine, Lana. You didn't mean to."

"I hit you, didn't I? I hurt you." Her eyes filled with tears. "Oh, Gabe, I'm sorry."

"Forget it, it's not a big deal."

She sat up. "Dammit, I thought I was through with the nightmares."

"Obviously you've had them before."

"Yes, but not in months. At first I dreamed all the time. Nightly, almost. Terence…" Her voice trailed off and she started again. "He moved out of the bedroom because I kept him awake. I hit him, just like I did you. He…he said I was dangerous." She sucked in air on a sob.

That rat bastard had said too damn many things to hurt her. "He's a stupid jerk. I told you, it's nothing."

She touched his cheek again, looking unbearably sad. "Maybe he was right."

"Don't say that. Don't beat yourself up over something you did accidentally. It's nothing, it doesn't even hurt."

"I thought I was better. Thought I was handling it. The self-defense course made me feel better. Safer. Stronger. More in control." She laughed bitterly. "I'm in great control, aren't I?"

Deliberately he grasped her arms. "You are better. You did what you had to do. Winters brought everything back to you, that's why you're having nightmares again. But they'll go away again, Lana. You conquered them once, you can do it again."

She got up and grabbed her pillows, then started to pull a blanket off the bed.

"What do you think you're doing?"

"I'm going to sleep on the couch. I'm not risking hitting you again."

"Lana, don't be ridiculous." Gabe grabbed the blanket and they tussled over it until she let go. "Come back to bed. Come on, honey, let me hold you."

He argued with her until finally she agreed. He wrapped his arms around her and held her close to his heart. Her head was against his chest and her breath was warm, though her body was icy-cold. He stroked his hands up and down her arms and her back, trying to warm her. Trying his best to comfort her.

"I don't know what to do," she whispered against his chest.

Neither did he. "Go to sleep, honey. We'll talk about it tomorrow."

THE NEXT MORNING they got up late and Lana had to leave for work, so they didn't talk. Gabe had a physical therapy appointment and after that he planned to go job hunting. Maybe even drive over to the employment office in Corpus Christi.

His phone rang a few minutes later. He checked Caller ID, surprised to see Red Covey's name come up.

"Hey, Red."

"How'd you know it was me?"

"Caller ID." Which Red didn't have because he considered it a newfangled waste of money. "How's it going?" Red was an old friend. In fact, he'd given Gabe his first fishing pole and his first job, working summers and after school at Red's bait and tackle shop in Corpus.

"Can't complain. How's that leg of yours? Must be pretty bad since you haven't gotten your butt over here in a month of Sundays."

Gabe grinned. Red didn't like to beat around the bush. "I'm doing okay. Tell you what, I have a physical therapy appointment this morning but I could come over there this afternoon. I've got some free time on my hands." And it would let him put off going to the employment office for another day.

"Sounds good. And it wouldn't hurt my feelings if you brought along a brew or two when you come."

Gabe was smiling as he hung up. Red was the one person, besides his family, whom Gabe hadn't been able to ban from his hospital room. But then, Red had been like another father to him, especially after his own had passed away. So that made him family in Gabe's book. He should have gone to see him before now. While he hadn't seemed to be slowing down, Red was in his mid-seventies and wouldn't be around forever.

Red's shop, located under the causeway bridge in Corpus, had one of the premium locations for the bait and tackle business. A large number of the locals fueled up there, especially the commercial fishing boat captains. Not that you'd know it to look at the place. It never changed, except maybe to get grimier. The sailfish on the wall was probably at least as old as Red, and to Gabe's knowledge, had never been dusted.

But Red was scrupulously honest, had the best diesel and gas prices around, and he was always willing to shoot the breeze with the fishermen who frequented his store. Over the years, a succession of teenage boys worked for him. Many of them, like Gabe, had gone on to become fishermen or successful businessmen in the community. Several of them, though, "weren't too bright" as Red put it, and the job at Red's was often the high point of their careers.

When Gabe arrived, Red was sitting where he always did, in a rocking chair on the dilapidated porch. The only thing that had changed was that his daughter had badgered him into quitting chewing tobacco. Now an enormous wad of bubble gum took the place of the chaw of tobacco that used to sit in his cheek.

Red's shrewd green eyes appraised him. "You look a sight better than you did last time I saw you. I don't mind telling you, hospitals give me the willies."

"I'm not real fond of them, either." Gabe handed him a beer from the six-pack he'd brought and opened one for himself, taking a seat in the other rocker. "I'm better. Not great, but a cane's better than those damn crutches."

Red took a deep swallow of beer, then burped. "Now that hits the spot." A companionable silence fell while Red rocked and drank. "Heard you sold your boat. Did you make a good deal on it?"

"Yeah. Better than I'd expected."

"That's good. *El Jugador* sure was a fine vessel. Shame you had to let it go."

"Yeah, it was. The buyer said you'd told him about it being for sale. Thanks for sending him my way."

He nodded. "Sure thing. So, you been thinking about what you're gonna do now?"

"Yeah, but thinking hasn't helped much." Gabe tipped back the can and drank some of his own beer. "Still haven't come up with anything." He looked out at the bay, at the rolling surf, gulls circling overhead in the bright blue sky. "All I ever wanted was to fish. And I had it." He glanced at Red. "But that's gone now. It's hard to realize you can't keep chasing that same dream."

"I reckon. You might think about chasing another one, though."

Like Lana. But he wasn't at all sure that was working, either. "I'm too old for dreams, Red. I'm mired here in reality."

Red gave a raucous, booming laugh. "Hell, son, you're never too old to dream. I'm seventy-five years old and I've still got dreams."

"So what's your dream, Red?" He looked at him curiously. He'd never heard Red talk like this before.

"I'm goin' to Florida. Open me another shop right on the ocean."

"You're moving? Leaving Texas? Why?" Red was a fixture. He and his shop were a landmark. He'd been there since…well, forever.

"My granddaughter's there. She's starting to spit out great-grandchildren and I've got a mind to see them. Ginger's been scoutin' out locations for me and says she's found just the place."

He still could hardly believe it. No more Red's place? Red, gone to Florida? But the old man looked happy, more than Gabe had seen him look in a long time. "Sounds like you've got it all planned."

"Yep." He took a sip of beer and nodded. "Except for one thing. I need to sell this place." He looked around with pride, seeing the place, Gabe knew, as it had been in his youth. "But I don't aim to sell it to just anybody. I want someone who'll treat it right." He speared Gabe with a sharp look and jabbed a gnarled finger at him. "So, how about it, Gabe?"

Gabe just stared at him. "You want me to buy your store? Me?"

"Why not? You said yourself you don't have any

plans. You can make a good living here. Always been good for me." When Gabe didn't answer, he said, "What's wrong? Think you're too good to be a shopkeeper?"

"No. I just never thought about it." But now he was beginning to see the possibilities. The place needed a lot of work, but hard work had never worried Gabe. He knew he could get some help from his family, especially his brother-in-law Mark, who had been in construction.

The location was perfect, and Red had a well-established clientele that would remain loyal to another local taking over. As long as Gabe didn't do something stupid, like raise prices too much. And it would be his own business, he wouldn't have to answer to anyone else.

"What kind of price are you talking?"

"I'll make you a fair deal. I don't gouge my friends or family."

"I've never known you to gouge anyone, Red. I'm just not sure I can afford it."

"Oh, I imagine we'll work something out that suits both of us." He grinned and crumpled his can and tossed it over his shoulder. "Now crack open another one of them beers and let's have a toast."

Gabe pulled a couple more beers out and opened them. "I can't imagine this place without you."

"Make it yours, son. It's time I passed it on." He took the can and smiled.

"To dreams," Gabe said, tapping his can against Red's.

"Damn straight," Red said.

CHAPTER TWENTY

GABE FELT GREAT. Better than he had since the day he'd realized he would have to give up deep-sea fishing for a living. Thanks to Red, he had something to look forward to now, a business he could build doing something he understood and enjoyed.

Best of all, he could even start fishing in the bay again. Red had included his 17-foot skiff in the bargain, claiming it wouldn't be worth hauling to Florida. Since the boat was twenty years old and hadn't been much to begin with, Red was probably right about that.

But the small boat would be fine for Gabe to use just for pleasure, at least until business was going well enough for him to afford a better one. Eventually he might even expand to take people on guided fishing tours of the bay.

He couldn't wait to tell Lana, so he stopped off at her house on the way back from Red's. He knew she was home from work because her car was parked in the driveway. He rang the doorbell and waited. Even though she'd given him a key, she kept the dead bolt on when she was there alone. She answered the door a moment later.

She wore a sleeveless pink blouse and the white skirt that made her legs look like they went on forever and set his mouth watering right off. Then he saw her face. She looked as though she'd been crying.

"What's wrong?"

"Nothing." She stood back to let him in.

He stepped inside and bent to kiss her. She turned her head and his lips landed on her cheek instead of her mouth. She tugged nervously on her skirt and wouldn't meet his eyes.

He looked at her closely but he couldn't tell anything from her expression. "You haven't eaten yet, have you? Let me take you out to dinner. I want to talk to you about something."

"I have dinner cooking. Why don't we eat here? I'm not really in the mood to go out."

"All right. But first tell me what's wrong." He touched a finger to her cheek. "You've been crying."

"It's nothing. A headache." She flashed him the most insincere smile he'd ever seen on her face and walked toward the kitchen. "Dinner should be ready shortly. Do you want something to drink? A beer? Tea?"

"No, I'm good." He wished he could say the same for her.

During dinner Lana was quiet and distracted. Gabe wanted to tell her about the shop, but she wasn't exactly inviting a heart-to-heart, so after a few attempts at conversation, he gave up. He applied himself to the chicken casserole she'd made, even though he wasn't all that hungry.

"Are you sure you're all right?" he finally asked her as they washed up after dinner. "Winters didn't change his mind or anything, did he?"

"Not as far as I know." She picked up the last pan to dry it. When she finished, she folded the dish towel and put it on the counter. "What was it you wanted to talk to me about?"

"It'll keep. What's going on, Lana?"

"We need to talk. About us."

"What about us?" He didn't like the sound of that. Especially not coupled with her behavior all night and how upset she'd been the night before.

She didn't answer, so he followed her into the den and they sat on the couch. Lana folded her hands together in her lap in a gesture he recognized as one she used for control. "I'm not sure how to say this." She plucked at her skirt, smoothed it down, then raised her gaze to his.

"Just say it." He was getting a bad feeling. A very bad feeling.

"I've been doing a lot of thinking since…the other night. About Winters, and how I reacted. And about other things."

"You don't need to worry about Winters. That's over and done with."

"No, it's not. And that's the problem."

"Lana—"

"No, please. Just let me finish. I've been thinking about you and me."

He'd been blown off enough to recognize the kiss-of-death talk. He just hadn't expected it from Lana. He'd thought…he'd thought she loved him, even though she wasn't ready to say it.

She took in a breath and said the words in a rush. "I don't think we should see each other anymore."

There it was. He should have seen it coming, but he hadn't. Even though he didn't see the point in dragging it out, he still had to know. "Why?"

"Our relationship isn't working. For either of us. We both know it," she added.

"Yeah, well I don't know it. Say what you mean, Lana. It's not working for you. Things were working for me just fine." He couldn't read her eyes at all. They were cool and remote, a gray-blue like the ocean in winter.

"Gabe, it must be obvious that I'm…not in a good place right now. I thought I'd managed to put my past behind me, but it's plain that I haven't. I need time to…figure out how to get my life back together. To figure out how I'm going to deal with the past. To find out if I ever can deal with it enough to have a relationship again."

"And I don't fit with your plans. You don't believe we could work this out together." He wouldn't beg her but, by God, he deserved an honest answer.

"No, I don't think we can. I need some time alone. Besides, I've already hurt you enough." She put her hand on his knee and looked at him earnestly. "I don't want to continue to hurt you."

He moved his leg away from her touch. If he could have paced, he would have. Hurt him? As if she wasn't killing him now? "Is this about last night? You're breaking up with me because you popped me one during a nightmare? Dammit, Lana, I told you that was nothing. It didn't bother me."

"It bothered *me*. But the dream isn't the only thing wrong. That's just a symptom."

"Stop making a federal case out of a nightmare. You had a bad dream, so what?"

"As if that were all, but it's not." She sprang up and started to pace. "It really bothers me that I misjudged a situation so badly I was arrested for assault."

"That wasn't your fault. If Winters hadn't been hassling you—"

"No." She shook her head. "No excuses. I should be able to deal with a drunk without breaking his nose."

"Maybe you overreacted, but that's understandable given what happened to you."

"This isn't just a minor problem, Gabe. I haven't

dealt with my past. I told you from the first, I don't know if I'll ever be able to."

"We can work it out," he repeated, knowing he sounded desperate. "If you want to."

"Gabe, I'm sorry. I think it's the best thing for both of us if we don't see each other for a while."

"Define 'a while.'"

"Gabe—"

"Forget it," he interrupted, and stood. She had no intention of ever getting back with him. She just wouldn't say it because she was trying to let him down easy. But there was nothing easy about this. Nothing easy about losing the one woman he'd ever truly loved.

Lana had never told him they would last forever. She'd never even told him she loved him. Obviously she didn't.

"I'm sorry," she said, and her voice cracked.

He still wanted to comfort her. What a dumbass he was. She didn't want his comfort. Or anything else from him. "Yeah, fine. I'll go get my stuff."

He limped out of the room and into her bedroom. He didn't have much. A few shirts, a razor and a toothbrush. He stood there looking around her bedroom a moment. It hadn't taken much time to rip out his heart. Get it over with quick, he thought. Before he made a fool of himself and begged her not to do it.

When he came back she was standing by the window with her back to him. He set his clothes beside the small table by the door. Then he got out his key chain and removed her key, laying it on the table.

"I put your key on the table. I'll gather your stuff together and you can come get it sometime." Preferably when he wasn't home.

She turned around. "I know you're angry. I can't blame you. I should never have let myself get involved with you in the first place."

He knew better than to ask, but he did it anyway. "Why did you then?"

"I wanted to be normal again, and I thought I could be with you. You were fun and you were kind. And you understood me in a way no one else could." She smiled faintly. "I couldn't resist you."

He laughed bitterly. "Yeah, that's me. Mr. Irresistible. I'm so hard to resist you can't wait to see the back of me."

"You have to know that's not how I feel. That isn't what I meant."

He shrugged. "Yeah, whatever. How about we don't dissect this breakup? It's over and that's that."

"Gabe—" She looked at him, her eyes swimming with tears. "I still…care about you. I always will."

Wasn't that peachy? She cared about him. Even now, when she was breaking his heart, he couldn't find it in him to hate her. It would be easier for him if he could.

"Do me a favor, darlin' and don't tell me you still

want to be friends. I've heard that line before and I never did like it much."

He walked out the door and didn't look back.

"FOR WHAT it's worth," Cat said the next day, "you're getting Red's place for a steal. I checked it out with Gail and she says normally those waterfront properties are very pricey. One she told me about went for nearly twice what you're paying."

Which—since Gail was a Realtor—she ought to know. "I offered him more but he wouldn't take it. I can't help feeling like I'm taking advantage of him."

Gabe had stopped by Cat's to go over his finances. He wanted to make sure he'd be able to swing the payments on the shop. He didn't feel very sociable but anything beat sitting home thinking about Lana. The sooner he and Red closed the deal, the sooner he'd have some work to throw himself into.

"He obviously wants you to have it, so I wouldn't worry about it. Besides, the place does need a lot of work. I doubt he's done anything to that property in thirty years."

"Probably not." He thought about what the shop and the docks had looked like the last time he'd seen them. "Make that definitely not. Where's your husband? I want to see if I could con him into helping me with some of the work."

"His mother came down and they took the kids to the Aquarium in Corpus."

"Why didn't you go?"

Her eyes danced. "Because this morning when they left I was throwing up."

He stared at her a minute, then shook his head. "You must be pregnant again. How many rugrats are you two going to have?"

"I don't know. This is only our third. We like having babies."

"Obviously." He tugged her hair and smiled. "Congrats, sis."

"Thanks." She gave him an exuberant hug. "You know with Cam and Delilah married now and having a baby, that only leaves you."

"Don't start, Cat." He'd been hoping he wouldn't have to tell her about him and Lana, at least not yet. He was still too raw to talk about it.

She started to say something, then looked at him closely. "Is everything all right with you and Lana?"

He didn't want to do this, but he knew his sister wouldn't give up easily. She'd nag him to death until he either told her or went crazy. "There is no me and Lana. We broke up last night."

"Oh, Gabe, I'm sorry," she said with ready sympathy. She put her hand on his arm and squeezed. "What happened? You've been so happy. I thought you two were in love."

"One of us was." But Lana hadn't been. Once again he'd been too dumb to see it. "Look, Cat, I don't want to talk about it."

"I think you do," she said shrewdly. "If you really hadn't wanted to talk you'd have glossed right over that question and left."

"Lana called it off. What's to talk about?"

"She must have had a reason. What did she say? Is there any hope that you'll get back together?"

"She said a lot of things, mostly along the lines of, 'I have to get my life together on my own.' Blah, blah, blah. But what she really meant was, she's not in love with me and she's figured out I'm not the right man for her."

Concern creased her brow. "What does that mean, 'get her life together'?"

He wished he could tell Cat the whole story. She was a woman, maybe she could help him understand what was going on in Lana's mind. But Lana had told him the story in confidence, and he wasn't sure he should break that confidence, even to tell his sister. Besides, what did it matter? Bottom line was, Lana didn't love him.

"She's got some problems because of…her past. And we had some problems because of that. I thought we could work everything out together. She didn't." He shrugged.

"Well, that's clear as mud. You can trust me, Gabe. I'm your sister, remember."

"It's not my story to tell."

"Does this have something to do with the night you were attacked at the Scarlet Parrot? I heard

Lana really did a number on the guy. Not that he didn't deserve it," she added hastily when he glared at her.

"Damn right he did. She thought he had a knife, and she'd been—"

"Oh, God. She's been attacked before. That's it, isn't it?" Cat stared at him. "Poor Lana. But I don't see why that would make her break up with you."

"It's a long story." He put his head back and closed his eyes, then opened them to look at Cat. "Lana was raped at knife point, two years ago. In a parking lot."

"Oh, Gabe. I'm so sorry. How terrible for her."

"She didn't want anyone to know. She said she was tired of everyone treating her differently and that's one reason she moved here. She didn't tell me until right after Winters accosted her. But I already suspected, even though I didn't know all the details."

"The other night brought it back to her."

"Yeah. She thought she was okay, but Winters coming at her, especially in a parking lot, freaked her out. And now she's decided that she needs time alone to deal with it."

"But, Gabe, that doesn't sound like she's through with you for good. She's confused and she's hurting. You shouldn't let her push you away, not when she needs you."

"You don't understand, Cat. I can't give her what she needs."

"She needs love. You love her."

"That's not enough."

"You're wrong. It's everything." She got up and went to the kitchen, bringing a couple of soft drinks back with her and handing him one. "Do you remember when Kyle Peters kidnapped me?"

"Of course." Peters was the scum that not only kidnapped Cat several years before, he'd framed Gabe for smuggling birds in an operation he'd been running in Aransas City for two years. But Mark had saved Cat before anything had happened to her. At least, that's what she'd said.

Gabe stared at her. "Tell me that bastard didn't—"

"No, no. Mark got there before he really hurt me. But Kyle abducted me, he held a gun on me and he—" She broke off, sucked in a shaky breath. "It's been years and it still makes me sick. He threatened to give me to the other smugglers and let them…do what they wanted to me. He painted a graphic picture of what that would be."

He clenched his fist. "And Mark let him live?"

"Mark didn't know everything when he found us. I told him later." She smiled. "Kyle is still in prison. Mark goes to his parole hearing every time it comes up to make sure he stays there."

"If Cam and I had known, he'd have been dead."

"Which is exactly why I didn't tell you. But that's not the point. The point is, I was a victim of a violent crime. Mark was there for me. He made sure I had counseling and he made sure I knew he wanted me. That helped me, Gabe, knowing he wanted me. Do you understand what I'm saying?"

Lana had to know he wanted her. Problem was, she didn't want him. "Cat, she freezes every time I touch her."

"She'll get past that."

"I'm not sure she wants to. Not with me, anyway. I think she had a flashback the first time after… And now she—" He looked away. "Damn, I can't believe I'm talking to my sister about this."

"Your sister who understands what Lana's going through. All I can tell you is my experience. And I wanted the man I loved to help me replace that nightmare with another memory. One of love, not violence."

"I don't know, Cat. It doesn't look like she wants anything from me now. She broke up with me, remember?"

"And you just accepted it, without even a fight. Can't you see she's confused?"

"I tried to talk her out of it, but she wasn't buying. What the hell was I supposed to do? Refuse to leave? She's done with us, Cat. She didn't give me a choice."

"I don't think you should give up on her," Cat insisted with that stubborn look in her eyes. "If you love her, you should fight for her."

"You're such a wide-eyed idealist. It doesn't matter that I'm in love with her. Lana doesn't love me. Period. End of discussion."

"What if you're wrong?"

"I'm not wrong." He wasn't about to torture himself hoping that he was wrong and that Lana would come to her senses. He needed to move on and try to forget her.

CHAPTER TWENTY-ONE

AFTER A WEEK Lana still missed Gabe desperately. She had nearly called him a dozen times. Only the conviction that she was doing what was best for both of them kept her from making that call.

That and the fact that he probably hated her for the way she'd broken up with him. He'd been so angry, so hurt. But she hadn't known any other way to go about it.

She hadn't called the therapist whose name Maggie had given her, either. In fact, she hadn't done a thing but go to work and then go home. She'd hardly eaten, she didn't sleep well; in other words, she was a mess. She'd told Gabe she needed the time alone to get her life together, but she was doing a lousy job of that.

What was she waiting for, lightning to strike her? No, a miracle to happen that would wipe out her past.

Disgusted with herself, she reached for the phone, but then she glanced at her watch. Nearly quitting time. The office staff might be gone for the day. Sick of her lack of action, she dialed anyway. If they were gone, she'd leave a message.

Five minutes later she had an appointment for the following week. At least it was a start.

Someone knocked on her office door. "Come in," she called as she wrote the appointment down on her calendar.

"Hi," Maggie said, poking her head in the door. "Your receptionist said to come on back and tell you she's taking off for the day."

"Hi, Maggie. How are you?"

"I'm good." She stepped inside and studied Lana for a minute. "But you look pretty down. Want to talk about it?"

Lana rubbed her neck and sighed. "I just called that counselor you told me about and made my first appointment. It took me all week to get up the nerve to do it."

"I'm glad. I've heard good things about her. I hope she can help you."

"Me, too," she said, though she had her doubts. "What can I do for you, Maggie?"

"I came by to see if you wanted to go to dinner. I had a date but he just called me with the lamest excuse to break a date I ever heard."

Lana smiled faintly. "You don't look heartbroken."

Maggie shrugged. "Easy come, easy go. Besides, I've had my heart broken. This guy didn't hold a candle to that one."

"That sounds like a story."

"I'll tell you about it sometime. After about three margaritas."

"All right, I'll remind you of that. Where do you want to eat?"

"The Parrot?"

That was the last place she wanted to go. "I don't think that's such a good idea."

"You have to go back sometime, Lana. You can't live in Aransas City and never eat at the Scarlet Parrot."

"It's not because of the other night."

"What is it, then?" Maggie took a seat in the side chair and crossed her legs.

"Gabe and I broke up."

"Everyone in town knows that." Maggie shot her a sharp look. "Word is you dumped him."

"I didn't dump him. I hate that expression. We decided it wasn't working."

Maggie pursed her lips and considered her a moment. "We decided? Or you decided?"

Lana frowned at her. "All right, it was my idea."

"You told me you were in love with Gabe. I don't understand."

"It's…a long story."

Maggie shook her head. "And I'm guessing you don't want to talk about it."

"No. I don't." Because she was afraid she'd break down and cry. Her emotions were so close to the surface, she was already near tears. And she was tired of crying, it made her feel like an emotional wreck.

"If you change your mind, I'm here."

"Thanks, Maggie."

"Are you worried about running into Gabe? Is that why you don't want to go? You can't avoid seeing him forever, either."

"I know that. I'm just not ready to see him yet. So it doesn't sound like a good idea to go to his brother's restaurant."

"Okay. Pick another place."

They finally agreed on the Mexican restaurant and left shortly.

It was early, so the restaurant wasn't too crowded and before long they were seated with their drinks in front of them. Maggie had ordered a beer and Lana a margarita.

"So tell me about your date that wasn't." Maybe it would get her mind off her own problems.

Maggie snorted. "A mutual friend set us up on our first date. We had a good time, or at least, I did. This was going to be our second and I actually had some hope for it. Cautiously optimistic, you could say. Then he called me out of the blue today, thirty minutes before he was supposed to pick me up, and said his sister had come into town suddenly."

"Let me guess, there's no sister."

"Nope."

"What a jerk."

"Yeah. I'm telling you, the dating pool around here leaves a lot to be desired." She picked up a chip, dipped it in hot sauce and munched. "Sometimes I decide I'm not going to bother anymore but then after a few months I try again. You'd think I'd learn."

"We always hope there's someone who'll prove us wrong." Like Gabe, Lana thought, and helped herself to the chips, as well. "Have you seen Gabe?"

"Not lately. Why?"

"I wondered how he was. For obvious reasons I haven't asked Jay."

Maggie was looking over Lana's shoulder and waving. "Don't look now, but you're about to find out."

"Gabe's here?" She panicked, wanting to see him, yet afraid to see him at the same time.

"Yep. And he's not alone."

Lana willed herself not to turn around and stare. "Is he coming this way?"

She had her answer a few seconds later when he stopped at their table. She drank in the sight of him, the dark hair, dark eyes and to-die-for good looks. Other than using a cane, he looked much as he had the first night she'd met him. As he had then, tonight he wore jeans but instead of his usual T-shirt, a blue, button-down, short-sleeved sports shirt. He must have been in the sun lately because he had some color in his cheeks.

Her gaze traveled to the woman beside him, a

stunning brunette who had to be fifteen years younger than him. Lana felt nauseous and hoped desperately that it didn't show on her face.

For the life of her, she couldn't speak. She and Gabe stared at each other in silence. Apparently he was as much at a loss for words as she was. Maggie, bless her, jumped into the awkward silence.

"Hi, Gabe, how's it going?"

He turned from staring at Lana and smiled at Maggie. "Can't complain." With the hand that wasn't gripping his cane, he gestured at the woman. "Katrina French, this is Maggie Barnes and Lana McCoy."

"Nice to meet you," she said cheerily, shaking hands with them both.

Lana couldn't stop herself from checking out the woman's left hand. No ring, dammit. Her heart sank even further, heading toward her toes.

"How are you?" Gabe asked Lana.

Terrible, she thought, *but obviously you're not.* "Good," she lied. "How are you?"

"I'm good." He nodded at both of them, then said to his date, "We'd better get going. 'Bye, Maggie. Lana." They moved away, taking a table that was, dammit to hell, directly in Lana's line of sight.

"Well, that was interesting," Maggie said, and sipped her beer. "Tell me again why you broke up? Because after watching that little byplay I don't believe for a minute that you're not still in love with him."

Lana gave a hollow laugh. "I hope he's not as observant as you are. He found consolation quickly enough."

Maggie looked at Gabe and the other woman, then back to Lana. "Maybe it's not what it seems."

Lana gave her a dirty look. "And pigs fly. Come on, Maggie. She's gorgeous. And young."

"She's pretty," Maggie conceded. "But he's not looking at her like he looks at you."

"How is that?" She sipped her drink, her eyes inexorably drawn to the two of them. The woman was talking animatedly and Gabe appeared to be giving her his full attention. He didn't spare a glance in Lana's direction.

"Like you're an oasis in the desert."

She wished. "He just found a newer, younger oasis then, because he can't take his eyes off her."

"Only because you're looking at him, I'll bet." Maggie sighed, sounding exasperated. "Lana, it's as plain as it can be that he's still in love with you. Besides, you broke up with him. Why shouldn't he go out with another woman? Why shouldn't he try to get on with his life?"

"Because I still love him," she blurted. "And I don't care if it makes me seem jealous and awful, but I don't want him to be with another woman." She wanted him to be with her. Unable to help herself, she glared at the woman.

The waitress brought their food. Lana took a couple of bites and put her fork down. It tasted like ashes.

"Why did you break up, then?" Maggie asked.

"Oh, Maggie, I thought it was the right thing to do. I couldn't ask him to wait while I gained some control over my life. You saw what I did to that man when I thought he was attacking me. I misjudged the situation terribly. I'm lucky I didn't hurt him even more."

"So? We all make mistakes. And Winters did accost you in the parking lot and get into it with Gabe. He wasn't blameless by a long shot."

"That's not all." She pressed her lips together. "I hit Gabe. I had a nightmare and hit him."

"Lana, you couldn't help that."

"I know, but it's another indication that I haven't moved on. That I might never move on. I need to be more in control of my life before I can have a relationship with Gabe. It isn't fair to him."

"Did he agree with you about that?"

"No. He wanted to work it out together."

"And you don't."

"I don't know if I can be the woman he needs."

"You're the woman he wants. Doesn't he get a vote?"

"He's voted. He's moved on. It's only been a week." An endless week for her, full of misery. "One lousy week and he's already going out with other women. I guess I'm getting what I deserve."

"WHAT'S GOOD to eat?" Katrina asked Gabe after the waiter brought their drinks and chips.

"I usually have Antonio's special enchiladas." Gabe was having a damn hard time not staring at Lana like some kind of lovelorn fool. Though he might be a fool, he did have some pride. He kept his gaze firmly on his menu or the woman across from him.

"I appreciate you making this a working dinner," Katrina said as she looked over the menu. "I'm taking the red-eye out of Corpus and wanted something more than cheese and crackers from the airport gift shop."

"No problem." She was beautiful, he admitted. Once upon a time he'd have been doing his best to get her into bed, business be damned. But that was before Lana had ruined him for other women.

Katrina closed her menu and laid it on the table. "I realize this might sound a little personal since I hardly know you and we're here on business, but why is that blonde you introduced me to looking at me like she wants to skewer me?"

"Is she?" Gabe put his beer down and glanced at Lana, who quickly looked away. Nah, wishful thinking. He picked up his beer and sipped again. "I don't think so."

"Oh, yeah, she is." She looked at Lana again, then back to him. "Does she have the hots for you or something?"

Gabe choked and set down his beer.

"Sorry, I have a bad habit of saying whatever pops into my head. But does she?"

Oh, hell, why not tell her? He wasn't likely to ever see her again, anyway. "Not anymore. We broke up a week ago. She broke it off."

Katrina glanced over at Lana again. "Doesn't look like she's done with you. Do you want me to tell her I'm just trying to sell you fuel pumps for your store?"

A sliver of hope kindled to life in his chest. If Lana was jealous, maybe she cared more than he'd thought. "No." He gave her his most charming smile. "Would you mind?"

Eyes dancing with merriment, she smiled back. "Anything for a potential client. Well, not *anything*," she added. "But this would be my pleasure. I've never minded flirting with a good-looking guy."

Gabe laughed. "Tell me about these new fuel pumps and why I should buy them."

She sent him a sultry smile and leaned forward. "I thought you'd never ask."

"I DON'T THINK I can stand this," Lana said, seeing the woman put her hand on Gabe's arm and stroke it.

"Dammit!"

Startled, Lana looked at Maggie.

Maggie's jaw tightened. Setting her fork down, she said, "Damn, damn, damn. I am *so* not doing this."

"What are you talking about, Maggie?"

"I said I wouldn't tell you but this—" She waved a hand in Gabe's direction. "This is beyond stupid. Do you know why Winters dropped the suit against you?"

"Yes. Gabe offered to pay him. I had to drag the story out of him and then make him let me pay him back."

"That's not all he offered him. The day after you were served, I stopped Winters for speeding. He had a ton of fishing tackle in the bed of his truck. I'm not talking a rod and reel or two, I'm talking a lot of stuff. Enough to outfit an entire commercial boat. He runs a charter service like Gabe does, so it was possible it was his, but it seemed odd to me he'd have it all in his truck and not at his boat. So I questioned him."

In dawning horror Lana said, "No. Oh, no. Tell me Gabe didn't—"

"Of course he did," Maggie snapped. "Winters made a deal with Gabe, the tackle and some cash for his dropping the suit. Gabe had sworn him to secrecy, but he sang like a songbird when he thought I would pop him for theft. I didn't believe him, so I called Gabe. It's true, Lana. Gabe made me promise not to tell you."

"Why would he do that? That tackle is so expensive, it will take him years to accumulate again."

"He's not planning on buying more. He won't be charter fishing again. He said he was done with it."

"For good?"

"That's what he said. He said he wouldn't be using it anymore anyway, so there was no reason not to give it to Winters."

"I feel awful. I can't believe he'd do something so rash. And not even tell me."

"He loves you. He wanted to spare you pain."

She looked at Gabe again. "If he loves me so much, then why is he flirting with that woman?"

Maggie rolled her eyes. "To make you jealous. And guess what, it's working."

Was it ever. "I could kill him. He shouldn't have done it. That boat was his dream. It was bad enough he had to sell it, but to get rid of all his tackle..." Because of her. Because he knew how she felt about going to court. He'd given up his dream without a backward glance.

"Can I be honest?" Maggie asked.

Lana smiled. "Aren't you always?"

Maggie's quick grin flashed. "My mother always said I was born without a speck of tact. I think—no, I know—if I had a man who loved me as much as Gabe loves you, I wouldn't give him up. Not for anything."

"I thought I was doing the right thing. Maybe... maybe I was wrong."

Maggie leaned forward and said very quietly, "Don't let the bastard who attacked you win. He's already torn your life apart once, don't let him do it again."

Lana stared at her. Was that what she was doing, letting the rapist win? "I hadn't thought about it that way. Letting him win. Everything I've done since that night has been in reaction to what he did to me. I haven't been dealing with it, getting past it. I've been letting that one night define me. And I've been scared. Too scared to let anyone close, so I pushed them away. Everyone, including Gabe. I've been a coward, but I'm not going to be one anymore."

"A coward is the last thing I'd call you, Lana. I think you're a remarkably strong woman who's had a terrible thing happen to her. And I think you deserve some happiness now." She reached across the table and squeezed Lana's hand. "And so does Gabe."

CHAPTER TWENTY-TWO

GABE'S TRUCK was the only vehicle in the driveway, but Lana knew that didn't mean he was home alone. She rang his doorbell, wondering what she'd do if the woman he'd taken to dinner was with him. She'd thought about calling first, but decided to hell with that. If the woman was inside, Lana was going in and hauling her perky butt out of there.

What if you find her in his bed? The nagging voice that wouldn't shut up whispered again. Resolutely, Lana pushed that possibility out of her mind. Although Gabe was perfectly free to do whatever he wanted, she couldn't believe he'd take another woman to bed so soon after they'd broken up. She wouldn't believe it unless she saw it.

Please, God, don't let her see it.

After what felt like eons later, Gabe opened the door. He didn't speak, just stood silhouetted in the open doorway, a dim glow of light behind him. He had on a pair of well-worn jeans, white at the stress points, zipped but not buttoned, and nothing else.

Bare feet, bare chest, tan male skin… Everything she'd been going to say flew out of her mind on a wave of pure, unadulterated desire.

His eyes were heavy-lidded, as if he'd just climbed out of bed, his jaw shadowed with his beard. His dark hair was disordered. From sleep, she wondered, or a woman's hands?

Her heart rate accelerated, her blood heated as her gaze traveled over his wide chest sprinkled with black hair, the sleekly muscled pecs and arms and the washboard abs she wanted desperately to put her hands on. Her mouth went dry as she dragged her gaze back to his face. She could tell absolutely nothing from his expression, which was as closed as she'd ever seen it.

"Is she here?"

His mouth lifted in a smile. He didn't answer, just stepped aside and let her in, then shut the door behind her. Yet still, he didn't speak.

"Tell me, dammit. Is that woman here?"

He jerked her into his arms and crushed his mouth to hers in a steaming kiss. Flinging her arms around his neck, she kissed him back, answering the rough thrust of his tongue with hers, plastering her body against his. His arms tightening around her, he kissed her with single-minded intensity.

Endless moments later he buried his face in her neck and held her close. "You have no idea how much I've wanted to do that."

"Was that a no?" she managed to gasp.

He laughed and nuzzled her neck. "Would I have answered the door if I'd had a woman here with me?"

The rush of relief was so intense it made her dizzy. "God, I hope not." She framed his face with her palms and smiled at him, her heart bursting with emotion. Suddenly nothing mattered, not the past, not all the hurt they'd both endured, nothing but the joy spreading through her. "I love you."

His eyes were so intense, liquid and deep, she could have drowned in them. His mouth curved upward and then he kissed her, slowly and very thoroughly. "I love you, Lana," he said, his voice as dark as midnight.

"Make love to me, Gabe," she whispered.

His eyes blazed and he kissed her again. Raised his head and said, "Come with me."

He'd lost his cane somewhere, but the big overstuffed chair beside the couch was only a few steps away. Gabe sat, bringing her with him, cradling her in his lap, his lips locked to hers. He tugged her blouse from the skirt, slipping his hand beneath to cup her breast and her nipple beaded instantly.

As he caressed her, she slid her hand over his chest and lower, down his abdomen, and still lower, to close her hand over his erection, straining against the denim.

They both groaned. He crushed his mouth to hers, tasting her greedily as she stroked him. He struggled with her buttons, managing to open a couple before he bunched the fabric at her sides and pushed it up over her breasts.

"Raise your arms," he said hoarsely.

She did as he said and he swept off the blouse, then popped her bra open and flung it aside. His eyes darkened to nearly black as he traced a finger down her breast and lightly circled first one nipple, then the other. She shuddered, wanting him so much she was on fire with it.

He filled his hands with her breasts, bent his head to touch his tongue to one nipple and then to suck it into his mouth. She felt the pull deep inside, in her very core, and her blood sizzled.

Raising his head, he gathered her to him, skin against skin, the hair on his chest, the hardness of his muscles, and the warmth of his body combining to send her pulse skyrocketing. She felt his lips at her neck and her head fell back. He feasted on her, sucked her neck, bit lightly and soothed it with his tongue, while his hands swept down her sides and then to her hips to pull her closer still.

Frantic to have him now, she wiggled away from him and went to work on his zipper. He fought with hers, cursing when he couldn't get it to work. She stood and shimmied out of the skirt, then slid her panties down her legs and watched as he pushed his jeans and briefs down and off. He held out his hands to her and she took them.

Lana straddled him and kissed him, sliding her tongue deep into his mouth.

He gripped her hips, positioning her above him, then slid home with a deep thrust. She moaned, tightened her muscles around him, kissed his mouth as their bodies strained against each other. His hands anchored her, caressed her as he pushed inside and pulled back, the friction so sweetly intense she thought she'd die. Her orgasm burst, crashing over her like the surf at high tide, spiraling out of control. He drove inside her a final time and she felt him come, her name on his lips as he did.

A long time later she was still sprawled limply against him, too content to move. "I was so afraid," she said, her head on his shoulder.

"What were you afraid of, honey?" One hand slipped through her hair with feather-light touches, toying with the ends, the other caressed her back in long smooth strokes from her neck to her hips.

"That you didn't want me."

"Lana, that was never the problem. I've always wanted you. I always will."

"And I was afraid I was frigid."

She heard the smile in his voice as he said, "Not even close."

She pulled back to look at him. Moved her fingers gently over his cheek as she gazed into his eyes. "Making love with you was wonderful, Gabe. But… it doesn't mean I won't ever have problems. Not every time, obviously, but I just don't know what to expect."

He turned his head to kiss her fingers. "Whatever happens, we'll work it out. Together," he said simply, and she believed him.

"I'm getting help. I'm going back to counseling. Next week."

"Is that what you want?"

"It's what I need."

"Then I'm glad." He tugged her head down and kissed her. "Have I mentioned that I love you?"

"Yes, but you can say it again. I love you, too." She started to kiss him but he stopped her.

"I have a big, comfortable bed in the other room. Think we could move in there? I'm afraid I'm going to be permanently frozen in this position if we don't move soon."

She laughed and slid off him. Held her hand out to grasp his. "You can lean on me."

"Good, because I don't have a clue what I've done with my cane."

"WE NEED TO TALK," Lana said a long time later. She was sitting in bed, wearing one of his T-shirts, though why she'd bothered, he didn't know. He liked looking at her naked and would have been happy to do it all night.

He propped himself up on his right arm. "Last time I heard those words, you broke up with me."

"I'm sorry I put us both through that. It was stupid of me."

"Doesn't matter," he said, taking one of her hands and bringing it to his lips. "You're here now and that's what counts."

"But it does matter. I should have talked to you. Listened to you. Instead, I pushed you away and put us both through a week of hell."

"Thank God, it only lasted a week. But you came back. What changed your mind?" He wondered if it had anything to do with seeing him with another woman, and if she'd admit to it if it did.

"Maggie said some things that made me think I was wrong. She said I was letting the rapist win by not allowing myself to find happiness. I realized she was right." She was quiet a moment, then said, "But that wasn't all. You should have talked to me. You should have told me what you did."

Puzzled, he looked at her.

"Gabe, why did you give Rod Winters all your tackle? That was a crazy thing to do."

"Damn." He sat up and leaned against the headboard, shoved a hand through his hair. "Maggie spilled it, didn't she? I told her not to tell you."

"Why? And why on earth did you do it? You know you can't afford to buy all new tackle."

"It doesn't matter, Lana. I don't need it."

"Gabe—" Her eyes shimmered with moisture. "You gave up your dream for me. It's too much."

"No." He shook his head. "I knew you'd think it was your fault and it wasn't. That's why I didn't want you to know. I'd already given up that dream." He touched her cheek, wet now with tears. "Don't cry. It was gone the day I had the wreck, Lana. I just didn't want to admit it."

"You might have been able to start over, if you'd kept that stuff," she insisted. "You still could, if you'd let me repay you."

He shook his head. "No, it's too late."

"Don't say that. It isn't too late. Once your leg is better—"

"I needed a break from my past before I could dream about my future." He took one of her hands and held it. "Giving him that tackle was a good thing, Lana. It made me consider other possibilities. I might not have if I hadn't been forced to accept that my fishing life was over for good."

"You sound happy. How can you be happy about this?"

"Because I have a new dream now. And I have you back. How can I lose?"

"You found something you want to do. Oh, Gabe, I'm so glad." Her eyes sparkled and lit up her face. "What is it? Tell me right now."

He grinned at her enthusiasm. "It'll keep. I'll tell you tomorrow, I promise."

"Why can't you tell me now? Gabe—"

He stopped her questions by kissing her. When

she would have spoken, he kissed her again. "Tomorrow. I have more important things to do tonight." He slid his hand to the hem of the T-shirt and started to lift it.

"Gabe, wait. There's something else."

He stopped because she sounded serious. "What?"

"I know I don't have any right to ask, or to object, or even to mention it…"

He smiled, certain he knew where she was headed. "Mention what?"

"That woman you were with. Was she…did she…would you have—" She broke off and glared at him. "Stop smiling, there's nothing amusing about it."

"You're jealous."

She narrowed her eyes at him. "And what if I am?"

He laughed. "I like it. But there's no need. It wasn't a date, Lana. She's a sales rep. We were having a business dinner."

She frowned. "You two seemed awfully cozy to be talking business."

"Because I knew you were watching. Katrina mentioned that you were sending her death looks and wanted to know why. So I told her. I figured if you were jealous maybe there was some hope for me after all."

"Oh, there was hope. I wanted to go over there and rip her hair out," Lana admitted. "I couldn't believe it when we ran into you. I'd avoided the Parrot purposely."

"Fate," he said, and ran a finger down her nose before he kissed it.

"What kind of a sales rep is she?"

He grinned and shook his head. "I'll tell you tomorrow. It's a surprise." He lay down and pulled her on top of him, kissed her thoroughly. "Tonight I have other surprises up my sleeve."

Her lips twitched. "You're not wearing a shirt."

"You are, though. But that's about to change," he said, and groaned when she wiggled her hips against him.

"You bet it is," she murmured, and kissed him.

CHAPTER TWENTY-THREE

"I CANNOT BELIEVE you blindfolded me," Lana said. "Or that I let you talk me into it." They'd been driving for twenty minutes or so, she thought, but she had no idea which direction they'd gone.

"I want it to be a surprise. As soon as we get there, you can take it off."

She smiled, thinking how excited Gabe had been this morning. They'd made love in the early dawn hours and not long after that he'd insisted they get out of bed and moving so he could show her his new business venture. Which he still wouldn't even hint about. She couldn't imagine what it was, but if Gabe was happy about it, and he sure seemed to be, then she was certain she would be, too.

The truck stopped. "We're here." She felt his hands untying her makeshift blindfold and take it off. Before she could see anything, he kissed her.

When she opened her eyes, she recognized the Corpus Christi causeway bridge immediately. Gabe had parked near a set of dilapidated docks that led to a small bait and tackle shop. An ancient, faded sign hung on top of the building that proclaimed it to be "Red's."

Gabe had one hand on her arm while she looked around. "This is it. What do you think?"

This was it? This…shack was his new venture? She thought it looked awful but clearly she couldn't say that. "It's…interesting."

"It needs a little work," he said. "Come on, let me show you around."

It needed a lot of work and she hadn't even seen the inside yet.

A sign in the window said Closed For Renovations. New Management. Her heart sank. He'd bought the place already?

Gabe pulled out a key and unlocked the door, swinging it open. He stepped inside and turned on the light, then waited for her to go through the door.

The shop was dark and dingy, overflowing with a variety of items, many of which she didn't recognize. She assumed they were some sort of fishing paraphernalia. There were a variety of smells, as well. Thankfully, she didn't recognize most of them, either.

A stuffed fish hung on the wall, encrusted with layers of dust and grime. A battered ball cap, equally dirty, perched on the fish's head. For the life of her, she couldn't think of a word to say.

"I know. The inside needs work, too," Gabe said,

limping beside her. He knocked a can off the shelf and dust exploded everywhere. Lana sneezed violently and backed away.

"And cleaning," Gabe added with a crooked grin. "Hell, I doubt Red cleaned it after his wife died and that was twenty or more years ago."

He was looking at her expectantly and she knew she had to say something and all she could think was why would he have bought a shop that hadn't been cleaned in twenty years? "When did you buy it?"

"Last week. I came by to see Red and he said he was moving to Florida and looking to sell the place." He looked around, affection in his gaze. "Red Covey sold me my first fishing pole. I was about six. I worked here summers and after school as a kid. Our dad would take Cam and me fishing nearly every weekend. Mostly, we'd come fish the bay out here. Guess that's one reason I loved it."

His dad. He'd told her his father had died about fifteen years before. "Sounds like you have a lot of fond memories of the place."

"Yeah, I do. Red's is an institution around here. I know it's not much to look at, but it's a great location. And people know the place."

"Well, it certainly is…interesting."

He smiled at her. "You said that before. You think I'm nuts, don't you?"

"No," she said hastily. "But it does seem like a huge undertaking to get it into shape."

"I can do most of the renovations myself and with my family's help. You know my brother-in-law Mark was in construction before he became a Fish and Wildlife Service agent. He said he'd be glad to help me, and Cam will pitch in, too. And I can take out a small business loan if I need to. Come on, let's go outside."

They went out and walked to the dock, to the fuel pumps. "The woman I was with last night? Katrina was trying to sell me new pumps. They're not cheap, but I'm thinking they'd be worth it."

He pointed to the shop again. "There's a new line of rods and reels I've been reading about that I'd like to carry. I'll have more room once I get rid of some of Red's stuff he's been keeping for thirty years. I still think I'll need to enlarge the shop, but that shouldn't be too hard."

She understood then. She heard it in his tone of voice, saw it in his eyes, alive with pleasure. He hadn't bought the shop because he couldn't think of anything else to do. He was excited and looking forward to the work. He was happy. She put her hand on his arm and squeezed. "It's wonderful, Gabe."

He looked at her and laughed. "It's a dump. But I have plans to change that."

"I'm sure it's going to be fantastic when you finish."

"So, you really don't think I'm crazy for buying it?"

"I think you're going to love it. I haven't heard you sound so happy since you told me what it was like to go deep-sea fishing."

"The minute Red said he was selling, I knew it was what I wanted to do." He put his arms around her and smiled into her eyes. "So, how do you feel about being a shopkeeper's girlfriend?"

She looped her arms around his neck and tugged his head down to kiss him. "I think I'm going to love being a shopkeeper's girlfriend. As long as you're the shopkeeper."

He kissed her again, longer and slower this time before he finally pulled back. "How would you feel about becoming a shopkeeper's wife?"

Surprise held her silent and she gazed into his eyes. She waited, holding her breath.

"I'd get down on one knee but if I did that I'd be stuck down there for good. So I'm just going to ask you right here. Will you marry me, Lana?"

"Gabe, I—"

He interrupted. "I know we just got back together and I'm probably rushing you. But I love you, Lana, and I think we could be happy together."

She put her fingers to his lips. "I would love to marry you."

"You would?" He stared at her as if he couldn't believe what she'd said.

Lana laughed and flung her arms around his neck. "Yes, I'll marry you."

"Hallelujah," he said, and crushed her in a bone-rattling hug before he kissed her.

They clung to each other, kissing and laughing

and kissing again until the strident sound of a boat's horn claimed their attention.

Gabe loosened his hold on her and turned toward the sound. "What? Can't you see I'm busy?" he snapped at a man in a small fishing craft who had moored by the fuel tanks.

"Well, pardon the hell out of me, buddy. Can't a man get a little service around here? Fill 'er up."

Gabe stared at the man. Finally he said, "We're closed for renovations. Didn't you see the sign?"

"I got to have some gas. How am I supposed to go fishing with no gas?" the man asked, clearly exasperated.

Lana dissolved into laughter. Gabe raised an eyebrow at her and grinned. "Well, Lana, what should I do?"

"Give the man some gas," she said, and kissed him.

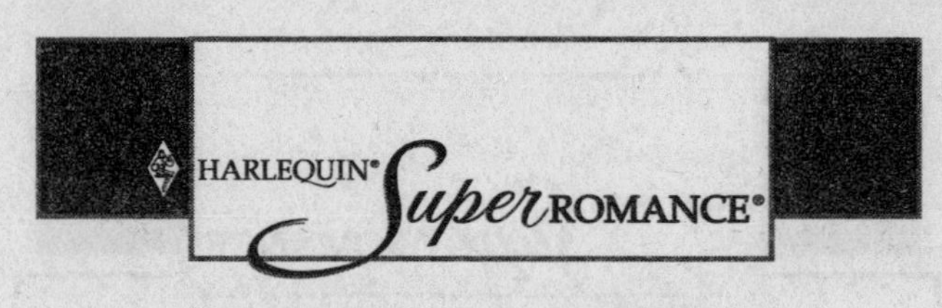

COMING NEXT MONTH

#1314 ALL ROADS LEAD TO TEXAS • Linda Warren
Home to Loveless County
With her three young half siblings in tow, Callie is headed for the safe haven of Homestead. Keeping her identity secret until the children's abusive stepfather is brought to trial isn't going to be easy—especially with Sheriff Wade Montgomery paying so much attention to the town's newest residents....

Home to Loveless County...because Texas is where the heart is.

#1315 A TIME TO GIVE • Kathryn Shay
9 Months Later
So what if Emily's pregnant with his child? She's still a traitor, and forgiveness doesn't come easily to Benedict Cassidy. If she hadn't agreed to marry him, he'd have fought the woman in court for custody once the baby was born. Instead, he's going to watch his wife like a hawk until he's got his child in his arms and his company back from her father.

#1316 MILLION TO ONE • Darlene Gardner
Finding the woman who might be her birth mother gives Kaylee Carter a sense of belonging that's been missing all her life. But Kaylee's happiness comes with a price. Sofia Donatelli has just won millions in the state lottery and Tony, her overprotective stepson, suspects Kaylee may actually be searching for easy money rather than answers. How can Kaylee convince Tony that love, and not money, is what drives her? Love not only for Sofia, but for him.

#1317 SHARING SPACES • Nadia Nichols
Senna McCallum and her grandfather never got along. So imagine her surprise when she discovers that he bequeathed her his share of a fishing lodge in the remote Labrador wilderness. Unfortunately, the lodge comes with her grandfather's annoying partner—Jack Hanson. In order to sell her half, Senna agrees to help Jack get the fishing lodge up and running, and then she can return to her life. But after a few weeks sharing spaces, Senna's not sure what she wants anymore.

#1318 THE GIRL WHO CAME BACK • Barbara McMahon
The House on Poppin Hill
When Eliza Shaw was sixteen, her life was torn apart by a lie. She and her two foster sisters were split up and she hasn't seen them since. Twelve years have passed and Eliza has returned to the house they grew up in to reconnect with the only mother she's known. But in going back, she must also face Cade Bennett, the only *love* she's ever known....

#1319 A DIFFERENT KIND OF MAN • Suzanne Cox
Count on a Cop
Emalea LeBlanc and Cypress Landing's newest investigator, Jackson Cooper, start off at odds when Emalea wins Jackson's prize Harley in a race. Emalea believes Jackson is the type of man she needs to avoid. But as the two begin working together, Emalea discovers there's a lot more to Jackson than meets the eye.

HSRCNM1105